# A Barren Landscape:

## In Search of an American Culture 1811 – 1861

### A Memoir of Eliza Rupp

# A Barren Landscape:

## In Search of an American Culture 1811 – 1861

## A Memoir of Eliza Rupp

### Geraldine Smith Priest

JoSara MeDia

A BARREN LANDSCAPE:
In Search of an American Culture
1811 – 1861
A Memoir of Eliza Rupp

Copyright © 2011 by Geraldine Smith Priest
All rights reserved. No part of this book may be used or reproduced in any manner whatsoever without written permission except in the case of brief quotations embodied in critical articles and reviews.

ISBN: 978-0-9843049-2-9

Published by:
JoSara MeDia
Tomball, Texas

*Cover illustration: The Connecticut River near Northampton, Massachusetts, 1836 By Thomas Cole (1801-1848), of the Hudson River School Source: The Metropolitan Museum of Art (image in the public domain as its copyright has expired)*

1st printing, November 2011

For

the two Dentons

# FOREWORD

From a lifelong love of history, music and the arts began to grow some years ago a vague but nagging feeling that I needed somehow to pull these things together. I had not a clue as to how to go about it until I came across a paragraph in Henry James' biography of Hawthorne which struck me like a lightning bolt and became the starting point as well as the pervasive theme of this book.

In a backward glance at a simpler time, when our New World seemed so full of promise, when our stresses were more limited in scope, and with an innate affinity for the beginnings of things, I have told this story of one family's struggle with what Henry James describes as a time of "a great desire for culture, a great interest in knowledge, in art, in aesthetics, together with a very scanty supply of the materials for such pursuits. Small things were made to do large service." Many, like James, found the American cultural landscape too bleak and spent their creative lives in Europe. To others, like Hawthorne, Longfellow, Emerson, Gilbert Stuart, Charles Bulfinch, we are grateful for a culture of our own. Has all their striving come to naught in our time?

In writing *A Barren Landscape* my aim has been to present a broad overview of America's cultural history in the fifty years before the Civil War – that great cataclysm that ended our young country's age of innocence. While the book is built around a fictional family, and in the format of a nineteenth century memoir, historical accuracy has been my primary concern; even the story of the Old Elm in Boston Common is authentic, having been found in a very old book in Boston. As for the paragraph from Henry James quoted at the outset, I leave it to the reader to decide if it seems unduly harsh.

To the authors of my historical sources, listed in the back of the book, I am grateful for a fascinating journey through these years. Most of the books I read were forty or fifty years or older, in many cases much older, finding them generally more descriptive and less analytical than more recent works. I am also indebted to the staffs of the Rice University Fondren Library, the Houston Public Library, the Boston Public Library, the Brookline Public Library, the Albany NY Public Library, the Massachusetts Historical Society and the Society for the Preservation of New England Antiquities for their ready and cheerful assistance. Warm thanks are in order as well to Professors Paul Cooper, Katherine Drew, Samuel Jones and Anne Schnoebelen of Rice University for their reading of the manuscript and encouragement at various stages of its birthing.

Finally, I express my special appreciation to my son-in-law, Steve, without whom this long-ago written manuscript would still be collecting dust on a bedroom closet shelf.

**Geraldine Smith Priest**

# List of Illustrations

| | |
|---|---|
| Broadway and Park Row, circa 1820 | 3 |
| Broadway from Rector Street | 3 |
| Map Showing Growth of New York City | 7 |
| Map of Eire Canal, circa 1840 | 13 |
| Henry Wadsworth Longfellow | 19 |
| Portrait of Washington Irving, circa 1809 | 21 |
| Portrait of William Cullen Bryant, 1833 | 23 |
| Interior of the Park Theater in New York City | 25 |
| Portrait of James Fenimore Cooper | 27 |
| Distant View of Niagara Falls, by Thomas Cole | 29 |
| Old Bowery Theatre, New York | 31 |
| Interior View of the Bowery Theatre | 31 |
| William Cullen Bryant with Thomas Cole | 39 |
| Packet Ship Passing Castle Williams | 47 |
| Bauplatz für Felsches, Leipzig | 49 |
| Clara Wieck, from an 1835 Lithograph | 54 |
| Portrait of Felix Mendelssohn Bartholdy | 56 |
| Portrait of Frédéric Chopin | 58 |
| The Leipzig Gewandhaus | 60 |
| Orchestral Score – Chopin First Piano Concerto | 64 |
| The Burning of the Merchants Exchange | 67 |
| The Primary Affected Areas of The Great Fire | 67 |
| Detail of 1852 Map of Boston | 75 |
| The National Lancers on the Boston Common | 79 |
| Ralph Waldo Emerson | 83 |
| Gilbert Stuart Portrait of George Washington | 86 |
| The Old Elm on Boston Common, circa 1845 | 90 |
| Harvard Alumni Procession, 1836 | 92 |
| Portrait of Nathaniel Hawthorne | 94 |
| Engraving of Margaret Fuller | 100 |
| Horace Mann Daguerreotype | 103 |
| Old Corner Bookstore | 112 |
| The Massachusetts State House | 119 |

**List of Illustrations** – continued

| | |
|---|---|
| Sophia Amelia Peabody Hawthorne | 126 |
| The Rescue by Horatio Greenough | 132 |
| Title Page, The Scarlet Letter, 1850 | 139 |
| Photograph of Herman Melville | 141 |
| The New Music Hall in Boston | 145 |
| Title Page of Uncle Tom's Cabin | 147 |
| Harper's Ferry Incident | 153 |
| Old Elm in Boston Common, 1872 | 159 |

*(unless explicitly noted, all images are in the public domain as their copyright has expired)*

... one might enumerate the items of high civilization, as it exists in other countries, which are absent from the texture of American life until it should become a wonder to know what was left. No State, in the European sense of the word, and indeed barely a specific national name. No sovereign, no court, no personal loyalty, no aristocracy, no church, no clergy, no army, no diplomatic service, no country gentlemen, no palaces, no castles, nor manors, nor old country houses, nor parsonages, nor thatched cottages, nor ivied ruins; no cathedrals, nor abbeys, nor little Norman churches; no great universities nor public schools – no Oxford, nor Eton, nor Harrow; no literature, no novels, no museums, no pictures, no political society, no sporting class – no Epsom nor Ascot! Some such list as that might be drawn up of the absent things in American life – especially in the American life of forty years ago, the effect of which, upon an English or a French imagination would probably, as a general thing, be appalling.

**Henry James**
*Hawthorne* **1879**

# Chapter I

Awakening as a child to the sounds of New York I remember even now with pleasure. I suppose it was my emerging musician's ear that somehow blended rattling wagons, barking dogs, and the cries of street vendors into a symphony of sorts. What must have seemed a cacophony of sound to most other ears filled me with delight, and often in early morning when the bedroom windows were open to the street below, I would slip from my bed, past my sleeping sister Emilie, to take up my favorite perch in the window seat. From there I watched and waited with eager expectation for the first sounds of gently tinkling bells, heralding sleek and pampered cows from the mansions of lower Manhattan as they made their daily amble up Broadway to the succulent grasses of Lispenard's meadow.

While my ears strained to catch the last faint sound of cowbells fading into the distance, my reverie would likely be jarred by the high-pitched voice of the chimney sweep on his morning rounds, crying "Sweep O! Sweep O!," perhaps followed closely by the Negro woman, red bandanna tied around her head, calling "White corn, white corn, get your lily-white corn!" as she and her decrepit nag passed below my window. Next might come the clam man singing "Here's clams, here's clams, here's clams today, lately come from Rockaway; good to roast, good to fry, good to make a clam pot-pie!" amidst the bustle and clatter of the awakening city's streets. When I finally had had my fill of the clamor I crept back to bed to await the stirring of the rest of the household, until the aroma of warm cinnamon buns and smoked bacon wafting up from the kitchen below lured me up for the day.

The bedroom that I shared with my sister was large and airy, papered in a rose-hued toile pattern much in favor in fashionable homes then, as were all things French. Located on the northeast corner of the second floor, it overlooked Broadway and City Hall Park. City Hall stood at the north end of the park at a right angle to Broadway, a proud example of American architecture at its finest. With its central portico flanked by two elegantly proportioned wings, its marble front glistening in the sunlight, I imagined it was a grand palace, filled with lords and ladies like the ones I saw in books in Father's library. But since America hadn't any lords or ladies, the nearest thing, I thought, must be the elegant gentlemen and their fashionable *femmes* that I watched promenading around the park on fine Sunday afternoons, while all manner of vehicles from splendid carriages to modest pushcarts rattled up and down the street past them.

This was my window to the world of New York City in the early years of the 1820s, years during which astonishing growth propelled her past Philadelphia to her undisputed place as America's largest, busiest and wealthiest city. The stream of immigrants from Europe at the turn of the nineteenth century had now become a flood. Sixteen hundred new houses were built in one year alone, and everywhere the city, echoing with the sound of hammers and saws, seemed in a perpetual state of newness. The masts of foreign and American ships were crowded like a forest scene along the piers and wharves of the East River, bringing to an eager population wines and silks of France, woolens and linens from England, rum and molasses from the Indies, to sail away again with cargoes loaded with American iron, timber, wheat and corn.

Our household in those early years consisted of Father and Mother, Emilie, three years older than I, the servants and me. I suppose that Peggy, our Scottish housekeeper, was more

Broadway and Park Row, circa 1820
City Hall is in the center, with the Park Theater on the right
Source: United States Library of Congress

Broadway from Rector Street
Grace Church Chapel is at the left and Trinity Church is to its right.
Source: United States Library of Congress

family than servant, for she was both housekeeper and nurse, overseeing Emilie and me as well as the household. Even now I sometimes at night remember her sweet voice, singing us to sleep with her old Scottish Highland ballads, their sentimental and romantic words by Robert Burns. Our Negro cook Esther and her husband Asa, whose primary responsibility was the care of the two gray horses and carriage, seemed to Emilie and me like family, too, for they watched over us with a firm and affectionate hand. Though they were both slightly stooped now and graying at the temples, there was no doubt who was in charge of the kitchen and carriage house.

Mine was a happy and secure world as I sat in my window seat, a child of seven or eight, enthralled by the sights and sounds of the bustling city below. Our house was large and commodious, but without any pretense of elegance. The shelves of Father's library held an impressive collection of books and prints, and there was a fine grand piano in the parlor. Mother had a treasured set of English porcelain that was brought out for company and special family occasions, but otherwise, unlike many prosperous New Yorkers of the time, we did not feel any particular compulsion to outdo our neighbors in the matter of possessions.

Emilie and I thought our father the handsomest of men, tall and erect, with extraordinary blue-gray eyes that seemed to me to see everything around him at once. We always looked forward to our occasional Sunday afternoon walks with him, for then we had him all to ourselves for a little while. The two of us were usually to be found upstairs in our room, Emilie with her dolls arranged around her for their reading lesson and I in my window seat, when Father would call from the foot of the stairs, "Emilie, Eliza, ready for a walk?" We would fly down to the hall where he stood waiting, smiling at our faces bright with anticipation. Mother saw to it that our hair and dresses were properly arranged, Peggy brought our wraps, and we skipped alongside Father down the front steps to the brick-paved sidewalk, off on an afternoon's excursion amidst the rattle and hum of the city.

Once on the sidewalk we turned down Broadway, in those years New York's chief attraction. Wide and lined with poplars, it was paved for a distance of two miles or so from the Battery at the southern tip of Manhattan Island to the outskirts of the city at the old Canal Street Bridge, beyond which lay scattered farms and meadows. As we walked toward the Battery we passed the oddly diverse structures that had grown up along Broadway, from one story wooden cottages to the fashionable brick or stone mansions of the leading merchants and gentry of the city. These were usually built in the English style, with iron grillwork adorning the front and the names of their owners engraved on metal plates on the door. In between were elegant shops whose windows presented as rich and varied a display as any in London or Paris: bookstores, jewelers, coach makers, hatters, linen shops, pastry shops, coffee shops, hotels; all were to be found along Broadway.

Nearing the southern tip of the island the haphazard design and lack of planning of the city became increasingly apparent. Irregular blocks were bounded by broad and pleasant main avenues as well as by dark, narrow, winding side streets, much like those in Europe. Father stopped occasionally along the way to speak to someone he knew, but presently our stroll would bring us to the Bowling Green, where a noisy game of football between rag-tag collections of students from Columbia College was usually in progress.

Emilie and I would wave at George Darby, the son of our family doctor, and laugh at the ferocity with which the usually reserved George played the game. Dr. Darby had delivered Emilie and me into the world, and lived with his family in a handsome red brick house just south of Trinity Church on Broadway. We walked past it on our excursions to the Battery, sometimes encountering Dr. Darby on his way to the hospital. George hoped to make a career of writing, despite his father's admonition that the law or medicine offered far greater assurance of a livelihood. Aware of Father's interest in literature and his friendship with the city's literati, he brought his essays and short stories to Father from time to time for his opinion of their merits. I suppose encouragement was what he sought; he never failed to receive it.

Resuming our walk to the Battery, we joined the milling throng enjoying this favorite spot for Sunday afternoon outings, watching with them as great ships, sails billowing in the wind, made their way out of the harbor, bound for some distant port. Two little girls, one dark-haired and serious, the other fair, with golden ringlets framing large blue eyes that seemed out of proportion to her small face, listened intently as Father told us again of sailing into this harbor as a young man from Leipzig, full of hopes and dreams and plans to build the same fine pianos in this new nation that had made his family name renowned in Europe.

In sight of the great guns of the Battery, Father, at my urging, would begin my favorite story, one that I never tired of hearing, about the "great celebration" of my birth on the night of February 11, 1815. He always began, "It was bitterly cold and the wind howled through the icy streets, but despite the cold the city was crowded with a wildly cheering throng; bells clanged and the cannon at the Battery roared. Torchlight parades continued all through the night and banners and flags were hung from steeples and domes in such a display of wild enthusiasm as the city had never seen." Then after a slight pause, he mentioned that it also happened to be the night that the nation first heard news of the treaty with England ending "Mr. Madison's War," signaling a new burst of trade and commerce that was to make New York the first city of America.

After the usual peals of laughter from Emilie and me, we turned toward home by way of Pearl Street so that we could walk by Father's factory and showroom located there. As we crossed Broad Street the foul odor from sunken gutters running down the center of the street, choked with refuse and home to barking dogs and rummaging pigs, seemed in startling contrast to the remaining old Dutch houses with their stepped gable

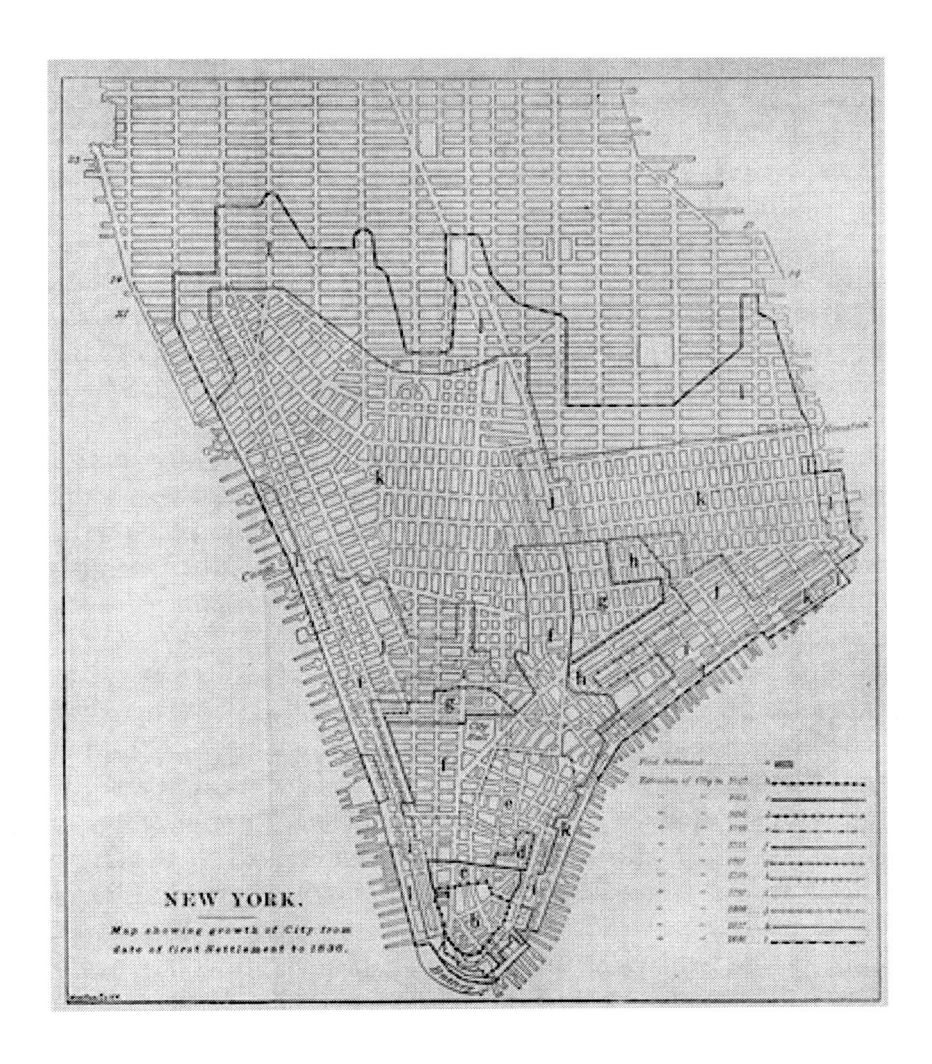

Map Showing Growth of New York City from date of First Settlement to 1836
From: Report on the Social Statistics of Cities,
Compiled by George E. Waring, Jr.,
United States Census Office, Part I, 1886.

ends to the street and their small colorful gardens in bloom. Walking faster now, Emilie and I looked eagerly ahead, past the businesses and warehouses along Pearl Street, for the familiar sign which read A. RUPP & SONS, LEIPZIG, LONDON, NEW YORK. Here, Father oversaw the building in America of Europe's finest keyboard instrument, the Rupp Piano.

Through the glass window of the showroom we could see shiny new pianos of various shapes and shelves stacked high with sheet music, most of it from the famous Leipzig publishing firm of Breitkopf and Hartel and including works of the greatest composers, past and present. Emilie and I had been born in the lodgings above the business, living above one's shop or store being usual then, and since moving to the large house on Broadway had missed our habit of running downstairs to visit Father once or twice during the business day. During the week a young man sat playing one piano or another for prospective buyers, while I listened wide-eyed with wonder at the glorious sounds emanating from them.

As we turned off Pearl onto Wall Street, I looked up at Father with my inevitable question at this juncture, "Father, when may I begin real piano lessons with a real teacher?", thinking that the scales and beginner pieces that Mother had already taught me somehow did not qualify as "real." I remember, all these years later, his smiling at the earnestness in my small child's face as he replied, "I have spoken with Herr Hoffmann about that matter and you will begin very soon." The sunset glowing red behind Trinity Church had never looked so beautiful as we turned onto Broadway once again. It was a tired and hungry little girl, blue eyes bright and cheeks flushed with excitement, whose footsteps turned toward home and whose thoughts had turned to supper.

Grandfather Augustus Rupp had already established his name as the premier cabinetmaker of Leipzig when he first turned his attention and skills to piano making. He had been born into a typical solid, industrious mid-eighteenth century burgher family for whom music was an indispensable ingredient of everyday life. In the evenings family and friends gathered around the clavichord in the parlor, while his mother played and they all sang from one of the many songbooks his father collected. The scene was the embodiment of German middle-class culture of the time, the instrument a visible symbol of the family's prosperity and status.

The Peace of Westphalia in 1648, ending weary years of war and destruction in Europe, had ushered in a long period of peace and prosperity, and with it the rise of a new middle class. By the mid-eighteenth century Leipzig, fortunate in its location at the juncture of two busy east-west trade routes, had become a thriving commercial center, creating a class of wealthy merchants and skilled administrators. Together with their increasing influence grew their desire for the accoutrements of culture: books, education, and music. Into this ready market flowed the newly developed fortepiano.

The instrument's two immediate ancestors were the harpsichord and the clavichord, the aristocratic harpsichord at the center of courtly musical life, the simpler and less elegant clavichord suited to the smaller rooms and more modest requirements of the bourgeois home. But by the beginning of the eighteenth century developing musical taste was ready for a more expressive keyboard instrument. The harpsichord, dazzling and showy, was incapable of contrasts of *piano* and *forte*, while the clavichord, its voice soft and sweet, produced a mere whisper of sound.

It was an Italian who is credited with inventing a keyed hammer instrument capable of producing not only loud and soft tones but gradations in between, but it fell to German craftsmen and the German cultural soil for the fortepiano to take root and flourish. By the middle of the eighteenth century wing-shaped, square, and upright pianos were being made and played all over Germany, and by the century's end its triumph over the earlier keyboard instruments was complete. From Germany the demand for pianos spread to the rest of Europe and from there to the New World.

It was during those waning years of the eighteenth century that Grandfather Rupp turned to building the instruments that would in time be acclaimed throughout the musical worlds of Europe. As soon as his four sons were old enough, they were put to work in his shop, learning every meticulous step in the construction of fine pianos along with their school lessons. They were taught how to select the best spruce for the soundboards, the tedious work of cutting keyboards, stringing and tuning.

Just outside the rear door of Grandfather's shop neat stacks of sawed wood waited, the layers separated by struts to allow the wind to blow through for curing, a process that required four or five years. Then the lengths would be brought inside to be painstakingly cut, planed, and sanded into the numerous parts before resting for another year or so in the drying room. Only then was the dried wood ready to be carefully assembled into the various piano shapes, the soundboards fitted and strung, the keyboards tuned, and finally the finished instruments waxed and polished to a soft warm glow.

Grandfather was artist as well as craftsman, with musical considerations always uppermost as his pianos took shape under his skilled hands and direction. In the beginning he followed the principles of the light-actioned German Stein piano preferred by Haydn and Mozart, but with the emergence of the great virtuoso Beethoven and his thundering crescendos, Grandfather foresaw that the course of piano development was forever changed. In the early years of the nineteenth century he began to add iron bracing to the all-wood instruments, at the same time crossing the bass strings over the treble strings, thereby strengthening the instrument and foreshadowing the great French and German piano makers to follow.

By the end of the first decade of the nineteenth century, from modest beginnings in his workshop in Leipzig with a handful of craftsmen, with his sons now grown and working alongside him, the Rupp piano factory had become the largest and most renowned in Europe. In 1810 the eldest son established a branch of A. Rupp & Sons in London to compete with the then-prevailing English Broadwood piano, and the next year my father, with his English bride beside him and ten Rupp square pianos in the cargo, set sail for America.

# Chapter II

The twenties were momentous years for New York City. The most momentous event of all, with the most far-reaching effects, was the opening amid much fanfare of the Erie Canal in 1825. The canal was the golden link connecting New York to the West, making possible the shipment of goods between the east coast and the interior at a fraction of the previous time and cost. A new surge of growth and prosperity followed in its wake, pushing the city's elegant residential and business districts farther and farther uptown, soon threatening even the rural retreat of Greenwich Village. Many of the old aristocracy - the Bleekers, Roosevelts, Knickerbockers, Stuyvesants, Van Courtlandts - however, continued to resist this northward migration, choosing to remain in their mansions down by the Bowling Green.

At the same time, the settlers of the Midwest had begun to crave the necessities and luxuries of Europe and the east coast that were available to New Yorkers, but most goods, like Father's pianos, were too bulky to be transported profitably by land. With the opening of the canal, Father's business, like all of New York, boomed, with Buffalo, Rochester, Syracuse and other smaller towns along the canal flourishing as well. Father's factory was barely able to meet the demand, despite his hiring additional craftsmen and sending to Leipzig for his younger brother Karl to come to his aid. Nevertheless, Father refused to compromise the Rupp & Son standards or painstaking

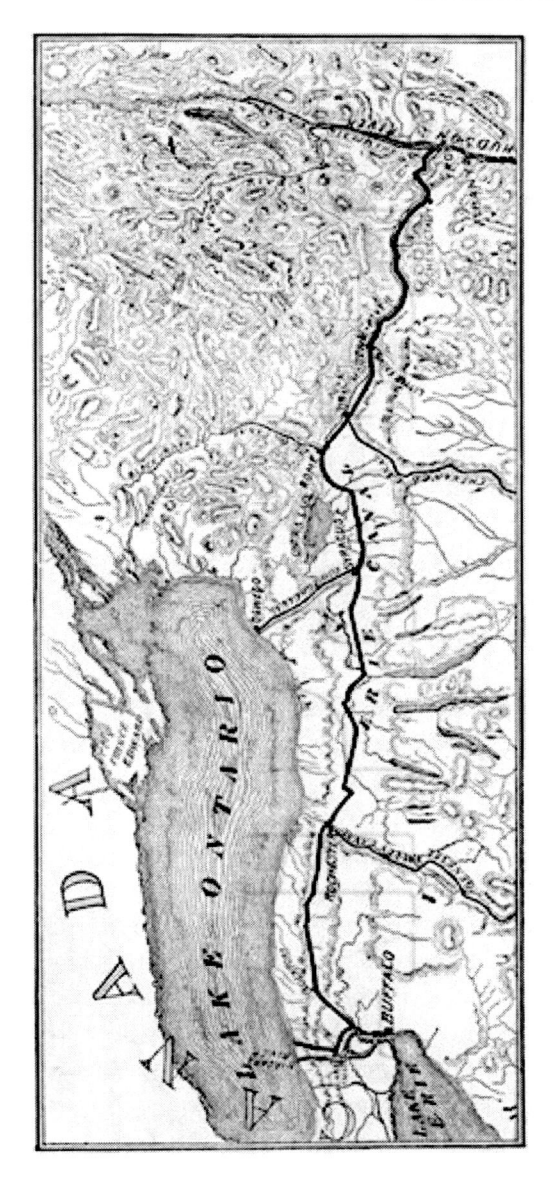

Map of Erie Canal, circa 1840
Source: Library of Congress

methods for the sake of producing more instruments faster. His primary objective, as always, was to build serious pianos for serious musicians and from that goal he never wavered.

He was aware, of course, that for every one of his pianos destined for the home, music room, or performance hall of a serious musician, that number many times over likely went to a Midwestern farmer for whose family it meant status, or to a frontier saloonkeeper who wanted to add a touch of respectability to an otherwise raucous establishment, or to a dilettante woman in New York or anywhere else who wished to add piano playing, even bad piano playing, to her list of "accomplishments." But Father remained philosophical, believing that any kind of music where none had existed before was the first step to a greater knowledge and appreciation of it, but in this, as in so many areas of American cultural development, he was over time to become quite disillusioned.

During these years he simply ignored the popular whim for extra-musical embellishments and tasteless ornamentation to which some piano makers turned, instruments on which were being played equally tasteless ditties with titles like "Pygmy Revels" being churned out by music publishers. But in the face of this cheapening of pianos and music, he remained, for the time, optimistic that for the public so enamored of the piano, genuine musical appreciation would follow.

There were, of course, other events during these eventful years which affected, often altered, the lives of many New Yorkers. Epidemics of cholera and yellow fever were nothing new to the city, nor were complaints about the filthy streets, especially in the older sections where pigs roamed at will. New York had always lacked good drinking water and it was generally believed that the brackish water and filth of the streets were responsible for the spread of these diseases. In our household, water that Esther brought in from the street pumps was used for washing and bathing; our drinking water was delivered by vendors who carted in casks of fresh, sweet spring water from the countryside. For whatever reason, we escaped most of the illnesses that plagued many New Yorkers, especially those living in the crowded older sections, for which we regularly gave thanks.

We had only recently moved from the Pearl Street lodgings to the house on Broadway when the first case of yellow fever broke out in Rector Street just below Trinity Church. Mother and Peggy, with Asa's help with the heavy lifting, were still arranging furniture and otherwise putting the house in order, stopping frequently to rest from the unusually oppressive early summer heat. As the days wore on the disease spread rapidly. Quicklime and coal dust were poured into the gutters and fires were set burning around the city in the belief that they would purify the air, but the death toll, despite all the efforts of the city fathers, continued to mount and by August all business of the city had been suspended. From my window seat the most usual sounds I heard now were hurrying footsteps of the doctors and the rattling of hearses through the streets.

Deep lines of fatigue were etched into Dr. Darby's face on the sultry August day that he came to our house to urge Father to take his family out of the city immediately. Father had already closed down his business, assuring his workers that their wages would continue until the epidemic had run its course. Although the heaviest concentration of the disease was in the area of lower Manhattan and residents there were fleeing by the thousands to upper Broadway and Greenwich Village on the outskirts of town, we prepared to leave at once. As one newspaper described the scene:

> Saturday, the 24th of August, our city presented the appearance of a town besieged. From daybreak 'til night one line of carts containing boxes, merchandise and effects, was seen moving toward Greenwich Village and the upper parts of the city. Carriages and hacks, wagons and horsemen, were scouring the streets and filling the roads; persons with anxiety strongly marked on their countenances, and with hurried gait, were

hustling through the streets. Temporary stores and offices were erecting, and even on the ensuing day carts were in motion and the hammer and saw busily at work. Within a few days thereafter the Customhouse, the Post Office, the banks, the insurance offices, and the printers of newspapers located themselves in the Village or in the upper part of Broadway, where they were free of impending danger; and these places almost instantaneously became the seat of the immense business usually carried on in the great metropolis.

The air was hot and heavy on the August morning that Asa brought the carriage loaded with trunks of clothing and other personal effects to the front steps, ready for the trip to the country house of friends, the Fieldings, where we were to remain for the duration of the epidemic. The drive northward along the Greenwich Road was slow, tedious, and dusty, the road crowded with every description of vehicle and humankind. As we neared the fields beyond the suburbs we were astonished to see an immense variety of temporary wooden buildings, having risen there seemingly overnight. Nearly the entire business section of the city had removed there; banking houses, insurance offices, coffee houses, dry goods, hardware and grocery stores, barber shops, grog and soda-water shops; all were busily engaged in carrying on the multitudinous affairs of the stricken city, as Father observed, without missing a beat.

By contrast, our stay at the Fieldings' was peaceful and pleasant. Mother, Emilie, and I took long walks through the fields and woods as the days turned cooler, while Father and Mr. Fielding discussed politics, the latest books, or the state of Mr. Fieldings' crops. Asa and Esther remained in town to watch over the house, seldom venturing out; Peggy had gone to visit relatives in Philadelphia. To my relief, the Fieldings owned a square piano so Mother and I continued my scales and exercises, while I longed for the epidemic to end so that my lessons with Herr Hoffmann might begin. Emilie, meanwhile, busied herself by holding school each morning for the three young Fielding children, who were noticeably less enthusiastic about the idea than she was.

While our family and friends thus occupied ourselves and the days grew shorter and the trees began to wrap themselves in their golden autumn cloaks, a young man was about to deliver his commencement oration at Bowdoin College, a small liberal arts college located in Brunswick, Maine. Stepping to the lectern in his long black robe, Henry Wadsworth Longfellow began his address on "Our Native Writers":

> Of the many causes which have hitherto retarded the growth of polite literature in our country, I have not time to say much. The greatest, which now exists, is doubtless the want of that exclusive attention, which eminence in any profession so imperiously demands. Ours is an age and a country of great minds, though perhaps not of great endeavors. Poetry with us has never yet been anything but a pastime. The fault, however, is not so much that of our writers, as of the prevalent modes of thinking which characterize our country and our times. We are a plain people that have had nothing to do with the mere pleasures and luxuries of life: and hence there has sprung up within us a quick-sightedness to the failings of literary men, and an aversion to anything that is not practical, operative, and thoroughgoing. But if we would ever have a national literature, our native writers must be patronized. Whatever there may be in letters, over which time shall have no power, must be 'born of great endeavors' and those endeavors are the offspring of liberal patronage. Putting off, then, what Shakespeare calls 'the visage of the times', we must become hearty well-wishers to our native authors, and with them there must be a deep and thorough conviction of the glory of their calling - an utter abandonment of everything else - and a noble self-devotion to the cause of literature.

> We have already much to hope from these things - for our hearts are already growing warm toward literary adventurers, and a generous spirit has gone abroad in our land, which shall liberalize and enlighten.

He finished his oration:

> We might rejoice, then, in the hope of beauty and sublimity in our national literature, for no people are richer than we are in the treasures of nature. And well may each of us feel a glorious and high-minded pride in saying, as he looks on the hills and vales - on the woods and waters of New England - This is my own, my native land.

As he returned to his place, there was one in the audience, a quiet, dark-haired classmate, who, upon his own graduation one year hence, would return to his Salem home, seclude himself in his attic room, and write, write, write. From Bowdoin these two classmates - Henry Wadsworth Longfellow and Nathaniel Hawthorne - would set out on different paths toward the same goal, not to meet again for several years.

The first frost at the end of October signaled a return to home and a more regular life, the removal of such vast numbers of people back to the city reminding one observer of the breaking up of some great army. It required a few days for our household to return to normal, but for me, the long-awaited piano lessons began and my life was forever changed.

Herr Hoffman came to our house once a week, beginning my instruction with the studies of Clementi and progressing to the sonatinas as he felt I was ready. I was so eager to master them that I spent every spare hour at the piano until Mother insisted that I needed more leisure time from school lessons and practicing; after all, she said, I was still just a child. She was right, of course, so I spent most of my free time in my window seat, dreaming of the day I might progress to the sonatas

Henry Wadsworth Longfellow,
painted by Charles Loring Elliott (1812 – 1868), circa 1842
Source: The Brooklyn Museum

of Haydn and Mozart, wondering if I dared hope someday to master the sonatas of the great Beethoven. I had often heard Herr Hoffman play one or another of these wondrous works at the occasional Sunday afternoon musicales that Mother and Father held in our parlor, with assorted friends and, always, Uncle Karl as an attentive and appreciative audience.

During these years, as Father's business continued to grow, so did his friendship with the city's literati. The success of the Rupp pianos in America gradually provided Father more leisure time with which to pursue other interests. He joined a group of men who met regularly in the bookshop of the cultivated Charles Wiley to discuss literature, art, and politics. Wiley had published the *Sketch Book* of Washington Irving, the acknowledged leader of the group until his departure for Europe some years before. The *Sketch Book*, like Irving's earlier *Salmagundi*, a witty satire of New York and New Yorkers, was eagerly devoured by the literate public and brought him a measure of eminence not before enjoyed by an American author. The primary object of the group in Wiley's backroom was to achieve for New York the literary and intellectual preeminence that New England had held in colonial times, despite the observation of more than one visitor that "New York is uniquely a city of business - one finds nothing unusual there in the arts or in literature."

Father around this time established an especially cordial relationship with William Cullen Bryant, lately arrived in New York from Massachusetts after achieving considerable notice as the author of the poem "Thanatopsis," published in the *North American Review* in 1817. This was followed by "To a Waterfowl" published less than a year later. Father wholeheartedly supported Bryant's views as expressed in this same publication in 1818, wherein he called for the development of a national literature of "genius, taste and diligence," rather than the "pompous pretensions" of many of our earlier writers in their attempts to copy the English neo-classicists.

Some years later Bryant would become editor of the *New*

Portrait of Washington Irving, circa 1809,
by John Wesley Jarvis (1780-1840)
Source: Library of Congress

*York Evening Post*, a position he would hold for many years, but for now he and Father enjoyed the camaraderie of the gatherings in Wiley's bookstore and occasional rambles together through the city or in the woods and fields of upper Manhattan, never too deep in discussion to fail to appreciate the beauties of nature around them. They were alike in many ways, more scholarly than social, with wide and varied interests and a passionate devotion to literature and the arts.

Father, having grown up amidst the rich cultural heritage of Leipzig with its love of music and books, was acutely aware of the disparity between European and American cultural development, but nevertheless, he was annoyed by the attitude of Europeans like British author Sydney Smith who wrote, "Who, in the four corners of the globe, reads an American book, or goes to an American play, or looks at an American painting or statue?" Father and the others of the Wiley group saw an opportunity for a distinctly American culture, but recognized at the same time that Americans, in their self-conscious striving for it, continually looked to Europe to show them the way. And too often, Father observed, they mistakenly equated wealth with culture; this was especially true of New Yorkers.

John Jacob Astor had arrived in America from Germany as a boy, and after years of trading furs for China silks and teas, had foreseen the enormous wealth to be made in Manhattan real estate. With the population of New York exploding and real estate values skyrocketing, he before long became the richest man in America. He, like other wealthy merchants, began displacing the landed gentry as the city's social leaders. They vied with each other to own the most luxuriously decorated mansions and to host the most lavish entertainments. Their confectioners, cooks, and decorators, as well, tried to outdo one another in presenting the most magnificent quadrilles and masquerades, often lasting until the early hours of the morning.

Their mansions were furnished in the latest Parisian taste, with gilded moldings, splendid mirrors, rich carpets, and elegant satin ottomans. The extravagance of their ladies' ward-

William Cullen Bryant, 1833
By James Frothingham
Source: Museum of Fine Arts, Boston

robes was described by one visitor as "quite extraordinary – twenty, forty, sixty dollars being paid for a bonnet to wear in a morning stroll up Broadway." During the winter season the ladies of fashionable society entertained with a constant round of dances, lectures, concerts, tea and card parties, balls and sleighing excursions, providing relief for the wealthy merchants and businessmen from the daytime obsession with trade and commerce.

The theater was the common denominator of all the entertainment in the city – wherever else New Yorkers' interests might lie, they all loved the theater. The Park Theatre, located on the southeast side of City Hall Park, was large and elegantly decorated with gold carving and red silk, and seating for 2,000. Its guiding light was William Dunlap, who presented Shakespeare along with his own unremarkable but popular plays, but he also imported the finest English players like Edmund Kean, Charles Matthews and William C. Macready.

Italian opera was first presented at the Park in these years and sporadically thereafter. Emilie and I watched wide-eyed from the window seat the evening that Mother and Father, dressed in their most elegant evening attire, walked across Broadway illuminated in the glow of the newly laid gas lamps, past the iron railing surrounding City Hall Park, to attend the brilliant opening of "Il Barbiere di Saviglia." Signorina Garcia, soon to become famous as Mme. Malibran, the most gifted and accomplished singer of the time, was the prima. As the glittering throng gathered for this memorable event in New York's social and cultural history, they must all have felt that New York was indeed a city of great promise. Where they differed was in what direction that lay.

Interior of the Park Theater in New York City
Source: United States Library of Congress

# Chapter III

With the arrival of country squire-turned novelist James Fenimore Cooper in New York, the literary scene was enlivened considerably. His novel, *The Spy*, published in 1821 had met with immediate success. The first genuine American novel, it was set in his own country against a backdrop of her own past, in this case the events of the Revolution. It grew out of his belief that America's past, however meager, afforded the same creative opportunity for historical romance that Walter Scott was finding in such rich abundance in other, older lands. The validity of this belief was borne out by the success of *The Spy* and two more novels of the same genre which followed in rapid succession.

Cooper promptly assumed leadership of the Wiley backroom meetings, which before long evolved into the more formally organized Bread and Cheese Club, so called because of the whimsical method of admitting new members: any cheese left on a plate when a name was proposed meant rejection. The club was composed of the backroom literati, the leading artists of the city, professional men, and political leaders like Congressman Gulian Verplanck, a tireless patron of literature and the arts in New York. Good food, good conversation, and good writing were the main objectives. Meetings were held fortnightly at the Washington Hotel at Broadway and Chambers Street with Cooper in charge, much like Washington Irving had been in the earlier, more informal days of the backroom.

Portrait of James Fenimore Cooper, 1822
By John Wesley Jarvis (1780 to 1840)
Source: New York State Historical Association

The common aspiration of this diverse membership was clear: to make New York the undisputed center of American arts and letters.

Among the artists of the Bread and Cheese Club were the aging John Trumbull, head of the New York Academy of Fine Arts, and a coterie of younger men who were turning away from the older school of painters with their European orientation, and looking for ways to turn art American: Thomas Cole with his unmistakably American landscapes, the landscapist Asher B. Durand, portraitist and genre painter Henry Inman, and Samuel F. B. Morse, remembered now as the inventor of the electric telegraph, but then a portrait painter of considerable repute. It was Morse who was chosen to paint the official portrait of the Marquis de Lafayette during his triumphal tour of America in 1824. It hangs still in City Hall, representing the crowning achievement of an artistic career which ultimately ended in frustration and disappointment.

In the mid-twenties most prosperous Americans believed that European art, like European books and fashions, were superior to anything American, but at least interest in art was growing with the result that there were now a number of substantial private collections of European paintings in America. In addition, a few prominent men were sending young painters to Europe to study, thus establishing the beginnings of a system of patronage. Still, the difficulty young artists and writers alike faced was expressed by Washington Irving when he wrote, "Unqualified for business, in a nation where everyone is busy; devoted to literature, where literary leisure is confounded with idleness; the man of letters is almost an insulated being, with few to understand, fewer to value, and scarcely any to encourage his pursuits."

In music as well, Americans were looking to Europe, with German music held up as the ideal. Like the writers and artists, young American musicians, those wealthy enough or fortunate enough to have a patron, went to Europe to study. The influx of musicians at that time had an enormous influence

Distant View of Niagara Falls,
By Thomas Cole, 1830
Source: Art Institute of Chicago

on American musical taste, with the German music teacher a familiar figure in cities and towns all over America. Their attempts to raise musical standards were often met with disappointment, however, as dilettantism in music remained the rule rather than the exception.

In the face of all this, Father and his friends of the Bread and Cheese Club remained firm in their belief that America need not look any longer to Europe as her cultural superior, that our new nation had her own unique materials that were worthy of encouragement, indeed must be encouraged if we were to escape a gross materialism in our rush toward economic and industrial progress. Perhaps it was as a respite from the ills of industrialization that the so-called Romantic Movement in literature, art, and music, having begun in Europe, spread to the New World, but whatever it was, Father and his friends recognized the necessity, even the urgency, of making Americans aware of the value of culture in making a society whole.

In 1826 another theater opened in New York which vied with the Park in size, elegance, and theatrical offerings. The Bowery was the first theater to be lighted by gas, it boasted the largest stage in America, and it paid Mme. Malibran $600 for a performance, an enormous sum then. The theater opened with a play, "Road to Ruin," which had a long and successful run. Mother and Father were part of the fashionable first night audience, Father having paid 75 cents each for box seats. At about the same time, Edwin Forrest appeared for the first time in New York at the Park Theatre as Othello, beginning an illustrious career as the most celebrated American tragedian of the day.

These two theaters seemed to satisfy, for the time at least, New Yorkers' insatiable appetite for theatrical fare; however, one event which caused an uproar was the first exhibition of French dancing in America. On the new Bowery Theatre stage appeared Madame Hutin, nearly naked, to the outrage of many in the audience; every lady in the first tier of boxes indignantly left the theater. The newspapers quickly joined the melee, the

A Barren Landscape 31

Old Bowery Theatre, New York, Opened Oct 26th 1826
Cigarette Trading Card

Interior View of the Bowery Theatre, New York
Published in the 1856-09-13 edition of Frank Leslie's Illustrated Newspaper.
From the United States Library of Congress

*Observer* thundering, "American women, let an institution that has dared to insult you be forever proscribed," yet another described a "respectable audience" witnessing the new "poetry of motion." Mother and Father, who were not present for the performance, read the papers with amusement and made no comment, at least that I heard.

At about this same time, I first began to notice that Emilie was mysteriously leaving the house every afternoon in the carriage with Asa, returning again just before supper. When I questioned her she did not answer me, and when I asked Asa, he told me to ask Miss Emilie. Finally, as I was coming downstairs one evening for supper, I saw Emilie and Father standing in his study; he was looking down at her and I remember how small and vulnerable she looked standing there. Father was saying, "Emilie, do you have any idea what a dangerous area Five Points is?" to which she replied, "Yes, Father, but the priest has given me permission to hold the classes in his church there, and Asa waits until I am safely inside before he leaves and I remain inside until he comes for me again." Father stood there for a moment longer, his blue-gray eyes fixed on her, then said, "Well, suppose you tell us about it at supper."

Five Points was a squalid area standing on the site northeast of City Hall that was once the Collect Pond, the pond having been filled in some years before. It was so named because Anthony, Orange, Cross, Little Water, and Mulberry streets intersected there, but its main claim to distinction was as the location of the Old Brewery which once had produced the most famous beer in the northeast. Time, neglect and the moist soil had taken their toll on the Old Brewery and the other buildings over the years, so that by the early twenties the area had become home to large numbers of poor Irish Catholic immigrants. At first, drunken and disorderly conduct were the worst problems there, but as the area deteriorated street gangs, thievery, bars and brothels became a serious concern to the city. Ignorance, poverty, and unemployment were rampant in Five Points, which genteel New Yorkers generally viewed as the natural condition of Irishmen.

Esther began serving supper as we took our accustomed places at the table, while I watched Emilie mentally preparing her case for Father. Perhaps because I was the younger sister I had always looked to Emilie as the strong and capable one, equal to any challenge, but now I had come to the realization that she actually possessed these traits to a remarkable degree for one so young. We began to eat in silence, unusual at our table, then Emilie turned to Father and said quietly, "I had intended to tell you about it, Father, but I was not even sure that anyone would respond to the notice that I put up in the church. But I have had fifteen or twenty every afternoon this week, older than I am, who are so eager to learn to read and write – that is all I'm trying to teach them. Mother gave Asa permission to drive me to the church every afternoon, then he goes on errands until time to come back for me, and he looks out for me very carefully, Father."

Drawing a deep breath, she continued, "You are able to send Eliza and me to Miss Fischer's for a fine education, and we are very grateful, but so many people in Five Points can't even read or write! If they could just read and write maybe they would be encouraged to send their children to school and maybe they could get jobs and maybe they wouldn't be so terribly *poor!*" At this, Emilie got up and left the room. Father called after her, "Emilie, return to the table, please, so that we can discuss this matter further and finish our meal." I looked down at my plate as Emilie, her face flushed, returned to the dining room and sat down at her place.

"What are you doing about books and tablets and pencils?" Father asked. "You know that the state has stopped giving funds to parish schools," Emilie answered, her eyes brightening, "but the priest said the church can provide a small sum for tablets and pencils and I will teach from my own books. Father Fitzgerald knows, of course, that I am Protestant and that I will teach only reading and writing as I have no cause to become involved in the Protestant-Catholic school controversy. I will use poems and stories that have nothing to do with religion and he is grateful for my offering to do this for no pay. Father, would you believe that crusty old priest waded into the midst of a riot in Five Points alone and was able to restore order!"

Father sat for a moment without saying anything, while Mother, Emilie, and I looked at each other, waiting for his reply. "All right, Emilie, we'll give it a try, but the first time you feel threatened or uneasy, that will be the end of it, agreed?" I knew then that Emilie was to devote her life to teaching in the same way that I already knew that I would devote mine to music, both of us unaware as yet of the difficulty of the paths we had chosen. As Esther cleared the table for dessert, Father asked if Asa still planned to march in the parade the next afternoon. "Oh yes suh, he'll be there, right up front!" she chuckled.

The last vestiges of slavery in New York State had been abolished on July 4, 1827 by a law passed by the legislature in 1817. The parade the next day was in celebration of that historic event, sponsored by the Wilberforce Society, a Negro organization of which Asa was a member. Visitors to New York often commented on the unexpected number of Negroes there and their apparent acceptance into the general population of the city. They were usually employed in service occupations, but many owned barbershops or fruit or oyster stands, providing a sufficient livelihood for them to support their own churches, theaters and social organizations.

The next afternoon Emilie and I watched and waited from the window seat, hoping to catch sight of Asa as he paraded by. Presently we could hear the first sounds of the band leading the procession as it approached, followed by a flag-bearer, his flag snapping in the brisk October wind, then the generally well-dressed marchers stepping to the music two by two. The officers wore badges and brightly colored ribbons on their chests, and one carried a blue box containing funds raised within the organization for the purpose of helping their sick and unfortunate brethren. Emilie and I at once recognized Asa, dressed in his Sunday best, as the bearer of the blue box.

He looked up as he passed by to see us waving and smiling from the window, his stooped shoulders erect as he marched on out of sight. For a quarter of an hour few but black faces were to be seen on Broadway, then the noise and hubbub of the street resumed apace, as if there had never been an interruption at all.

In these waning years of the twenties the business of New York was still booming, Father and Uncle Karl were as busy as ever, John Jacob Astor was wealthier than ever, and most prosperous New Yorkers seemed to view this as the city's perpetual state. The mansions were showier, the ladies' wardrobes more extravagant, the balls more magnificent, the streets and docks noisier, and learning and the arts continued to play a secondary role to amusement and entertainment, which continued to flourish with the ever-increasing commercial wealth. Peggy married and moved to her own home, but she still came in every day to help Mother in running the household, and still sang her lovely Highland songs for us if we asked.

Father still went regularly to the Bread and Cheese Club, but the now famous Fenimore Cooper and his family had left for Europe for an extended stay, leaving the group without its driving force. George Darby had graduated from Columbia and had gone to live in Boston, expecting to find a more congenial atmosphere for his writing than the frenzied pace of New York offered. In 1829, Father's friend and now the most noted poet in the country, Cullen Bryant, became editor of the *New York Evening Post*. In those days, newspaper editors also functioned as spokesmen for political parties, and the lament by the *New England Magazine* that "With the same hand that wrote 'To a Waterfowl' he was scrawling political paragraphs and offered no longer to nature, upon her mountain altars, a sacrifice of song" was shared by many of his friends. The young poet John Greenleaf Whittier was even more distressed by Bryant's "daily twaddle" of factional politics and expressed his unhappiness in a poem:

>     Men have looked up to thee, as one to be
>     A portion of our glory; and the light
>     And fairy hands of woman beckoning thee
>     On to thy laurel guerdon; and those bright
>     And gifted spirits, whom the broad blue sea
>     Hath shut from thy communion, bid thee, "Write",
>     Like John of Patmos.  Is all this forgotten,
>     For Yankee brawls and Carolina cotton?

Bryant's reply to these protestations was that he had chosen "politics and a belly-full to poetry and starvation."

## Chapter IV

It was becoming increasingly clear as the twenties retreated into history that New York's aspirations to become the intellectual center of America had not been realized, and by 1830 New England once again assumed the leadership role in these affairs that it had played in colonial times. But the fevered tempo of trade and commerce continued unabated. Enormous prices were being paid for property in the once fashionable lower sections of the city as residents moved to the upper areas, the homes they vacated being rapidly converted into businesses. Even John Jacob Astor's mansion on Broadway between Vesey and Barclay streets was soon to be demolished to make way for the 600 room Astor House, to occupy the entire block and to be the most elegant hotel in New York, or anywhere else in the country.

Our treasured Sunday afternoon strolls with Father continued, but now as we made our way down Broadway to the Battery our view was becoming increasingly cluttered by signs, awnings, and colorful playbills hanging above our heads, so that the street had begun to take on something of a carnival aspect. The traffic and noise had grown to such a din that my ears, now thoroughly attuned to the beauties of Haydn, Mozart, and Beethoven, felt assaulted. No longer did I take any pleasure in the activity of the streets, and no longer did I awaken to the sound of gently tinkling cowbells, for now Lispenard's meadow had been swallowed up in the relentless northward march of the city.

In 1832 Washington Irving returned from his long odyssey in Europe to a festive dinner given in his honor at the City Hotel. Father was among the large and distinguished gathering which welcomed home the first American author to achieve renown in Europe as well as in his own country. Fenimore Cooper, having left for Europe in 1826 as something of a national hero, returned in 1833 to find, however, that his popularity had waned, his later books with European settings not well received by either the critics or the public. His years abroad had left him with the opinion that America was not living up to her promise, and he lamented what he perceived as a decline in his country's manners, morals, and national spirit during his absence.

At the same time, Cullen Bryant was finding himself, as editor of the *Evening Post*, increasingly drawn into the political quarrels of the day, with political debates with editors of rival newspapers occupying much of his time and thought. But still he saw to it that the plays at the Park and the Bowery were reviewed at length, and that articles about the city's artists and the exhibitions at the National Academy of Art appeared regularly. He continued his stalwart defense of American art, writing that America's artists were equal to any in Europe, with "mountains and clouds, earth and skies as fitted to inspire the poet or the painter as Italy can boast."

The press of responsibilities at the Post forced him finally to give up poetry altogether, but he did find time to select eighty-eight of his verses for a volume to be published here and in England. His poems had appeared in various publications over the years, but this was the first time they had been gathered into book form. He was gratified by the reception his book received in America, even more so by its reception in England, underscoring his recognition as his country's foremost poet.

My lessons with Herr Hoffmann continued through these years with few interruptions, and he was satisfied enough with my progress that now I was a regular performer not only at the

A Barren Landscape   39

A Painting by Asher Brown Durand,
showing William Cullen Bryant with Thomas Cole,
in this Hudson River School work
Source: United States Library of Congress

Sunday afternoon musicales in our parlor, but in the homes of some of New York's leading citizens as well. Father would not allow me to perform in public, and for now I accepted that restriction without question. Only once or twice did I experience a frightening lapse of memory before an audience, but Herr Hoffmann had taught me to improvise in such situations so that few, if any, listeners were aware that there might be a few measures of Eliza Rupp mixed into the Frederic Chopin.

The new fashion for playing from memory had begun with Chopin and Liszt in Paris, where they were dazzling audiences not only with their prodigious piano techniques but with their prodigious memories as well. Letters from Father's brothers in Europe kept us abreast of these musical developments in general and, in particular, those of interest in Leipzig. Father's remaining brother in Leipzig, Uncle Hugo, was especially enthusiastic about a young Leipzig fraulein by the name of Clara Wieck, such a prodigy that her father was also becoming famous as her teacher. She was already at age thirteen booked for winter subscription concerts in the Leipzig Gewandhaus for performances of major concertos with their excellent orchestra. Before long his letters began to suggest to Father that I be allowed to come to Leipzig to study for a year or two with Friedrich Wieck, at the same time absorbing life in one of the most culturally rich cities of Europe.

To my young and impressionable mind the idea seemed almost too exciting to comprehend, and I pored and cried over every letter until they were smudged and stained and very nearly illegible. But now that I practiced with the possibility of studying with the famous Herr Wieck before me, my fingers grew ever more confident and my repertoire ever larger. My programs at the Sunday musicales might now include, along with Haydn, Mozart, and Beethoven, the solo piano pieces of such contemporaries as Kalkbrenner, Chopin, Schubert, or Schumann, together with an occasional Mozart sonata for violin and piano played with a violinist friend of Herr Hoffmann's. There was nothing of Liszt's in my repertoire yet as

Herr Hoffmann felt his showy virtuoso pieces were not suitable for me.

On one of our Sunday afternoon strolls in the early autumn of 1834, Father seemed unusually quiet as we neared the Battery, listening to the chanty singing of the crew of a great sailing ship as she pulled gracefully up to a pier. Emilie and I stood there in the soft warm sunshine while the breeze from the harbor blew our skirts and hair gently about as it had done on so many Sunday afternoons before. Father presently turned to me, and looking at me quite seriously, said, "Eliza, your Uncle Karl and I have been discussing the matter of your going to Leipzig to study and we have decided that he will accompany you there early next summer. I have already written to your Uncle Hugo to tell him of our plans. This should give us ample time to make the necessary preparations for the trip."

I stood there as if thunderstruck for a moment, scarcely believing what my ears had heard, then Emilie and I both threw our arms around his neck, laughing and crying at the same time. "Now I suggest that we get a carriage to go home as quickly as we can so that you can tell your mother the news," Father said as he handed me his handkerchief. I turned to look toward the harbor once again, trembling at the realization that in a few short months I would be boarding one of the sleek packet ships that I had watched so many times coming and going, taking passengers to and from foreign places that I had only read or heard about.

I cried into Father's handkerchief all the way home, then Emilie and I jumped out of the carriage and ran through the door and into the parlor where Mother sat reading in her favorite chair by the window. I blurted out the news and in the midst of the crying and hugging Esther and Asa appeared in the doorway with anxious expressions, alarmed at the scene they were witnessing. I ran to share the excitement with them, whereupon they laughed and cried too, before hurrying off, at Father's request, to fetch a bottle of his best wine and Mother's most elegant crystal glasses.

## Chapter V

Emilie was now almost as well known in Five Points as Father Fitzgerald, for she taught several classes for children as well as adults, remaining true to her pledge to teach only reading and writing and to stay out of the ever-boiling school funding waters.

In 1805 a public school system for New York City had been organized, called the Free School Society, to provide education for poor children who were not provided for by church schools. At the same time state funds were given to the Society to distribute to both Protestant and Catholic schools, but abuses caused the state in 1825 to cease funding these schools, with the result that by the thirties almost half of the children in the city did not attend school at all. Most Catholics refused to send their children to public schools because Protestant Bibles were used and they considered their textbooks anti-Catholic, thus the appalling state of illiteracy that existed in Five Points.

As I watched and listened to Emilie during supper each night, recounting some small measure of success in her afternoon's endeavor, I thought that she was surely destined to make her mark in the world. She was shining a thin pale beam of light into an almost overwhelming darkness of ignorance and poverty, but she had the strength and determination to persevere day after day when success was measured in slow and tiny increments. Then I thought of myself, lacking her strength, but no less fervent in my passion to bring beauty where she brought light. But I knew that light must come first - she was the one to forge ahead, I to follow behind with a gentler message for anyone ready to receive it.

The world needed her work before it would be ready for mine, but I was patient and willing to wait for as long as it required. After the world was earning a living, sleeping in warm beds with full stomachs, then they would welcome what I had to offer. But would that time ever really come? It seemed to me that even with warm beds and full stomachs they turned to other pursuits and pleasures. No matter. I would do what I had to do, never pausing to measure success at all.

It was increasingly clear to Emilie and me, meanwhile, that Father was becoming more and more disillusioned with life in New York City. He had already received several quite profitable offers for our house as business encroached farther and farther up Broadway. Occasionally during supper he and Mother discussed the possibility of moving the family to Boston; Uncle Karl was certainly capable of running the business, and Father was thinking that perhaps he could retire to Boston and devote himself to his literary and other interests in a more intellectually stimulating and less harried environment. He and Mother suggested that Emilie could open a school there and, at least, would be paid for her teaching. As for me, they expected that I would have as many, if not more, performing opportunities there as in New York, especially once it became known that I had studied with the famous Frederick Wieck in Europe. I doubt, however, that it had ever occurred to either of them that I might also hope to make my own way as a concert artist.

Emilie and I agreed, in our talks later in our room, that adding to Father's discontent was the demise of the Bread and Cheese Club, with the fellowship of interesting friends that it had afforded him. But even more so, we thought, was the departure of Cullen Bryant and his family for Europe in 1834. There was no question that Father missed the countryside rambles and conversations with his friend, which had continued despite the heavy weight of Bryant's editorial duties. For the time being, however, all their plans were nothing more than speculation, for our more immediate concern was to make the necessary preparations for the departure only a few months hence of Uncle Karl and me. The plans would have to await, in any event, Uncle Karl's return from Europe.

As the winter progressed, Mother and I busied ourselves with assembling a wardrobe sufficient for a year's sojourn abroad, while Father and Uncle Karl booked passage for us on the packet ship *Aurora* departing New York on June 4. Herr Hoffmann and I worked to bring my repertoire up to performing level as, of course, I would have to audition for Herr Wieck as a prerequisite for acceptance by him as a pupil. Adding to the whirl of activity, friends came by regularly to share in the excitement of my upcoming adventure and to wish me *bon voyage*.

Our happiness was clouded that bitter cold February, however, when Mother fell ill with what Dr. Darby diagnosed as pneumonia. None of us had ever had any serious illnesses, so worry and concern weighed heavily on our household. Though small and delicate looking with her porcelain skin and chestnut hair, Mother was, in her gentle English way, a strong and capable woman, tending to her responsibilities with quiet grace and intelligence. She was a woman complete and fulfilled in her love for our father, in the management of his household, and in the care and nurturing of his children.

She was friend, mistress, and gracious hostess to him, teacher, example, and confidante to Emilie and me. She had never been taken for granted, yet it had never occurred to any of us that there could come a time when she would not be there for us. Father knew, too, that as strong as he was, he leaned on her in many ways and could not have achieved the success that he had had without the domestic peace, comfort, and happiness that she provided. Thus the one good thing that came out of her illness was that we told her these things.

By spring Mother was up and about as usual and we were

busy once again with final preparations for my departure. The trunks were carefully packed with clothing for all seasons, while Herr Hoffmann and I continued to work at the piano, going over the most difficult pieces again and again. I felt exhilarated to have them so under control, and wished that I had not such a long time to wait to play them for Herr Wieck. My dear teacher could barely conceal his excitement, as much as he tried, and made me promise to write him about every musical happening in Leipzig.

The long-awaited day finally arrived, a beautiful clear and sunny day that I thought to be a good omen. Asa loaded the trunks onto the carriage, where they occupied so much space that Father hired another to accommodate the entourage that accompanied Uncle Karl and me to the docks. Esther had packed each of us a basket of fruit and sweets for the first few days at sea, but in her excitement had left them in the carriage. Hurrying off to retrieve them, she returned in a few moments and as I thanked her, the familiar aroma of freshly baked cinnamon buns made me realize for the first time, I think, how much I had always taken for granted.

Sailing days were always festive events in New York, with crowds of enthusiastic well-wishers gathered to see friends or loved ones off. Others were there to see to the loading of valuable merchandise bound for some foreign market. But all were thrilled by the sight of a packet ship as her sails filled and she turned slowly on her heel to the accompanying chanty singing of the crewmen, the sound of which could be heard all over the Battery and well up into Broadway.

As the passengers began to board, a sudden, unexpected wave of sadness swept over me and tears streamed down my face as I bade farewell to my assembled family and friends. For a young woman of twenty who had never been away from home for more than a few days, a year seemed a long time indeed, but Uncle Karl took my hand and the sadness was gone as we turned to join the other passengers. When the *Aurora* finished boarding she dropped down the East River and anchored off the Battery to await a favorable tide. As the flood tide slackened, the ship turned to the wind and we were underway, and I was comforted knowing that those on shore could hear the chanty singing too.

Packet Ship Passing Castle Williams,
New York Harbor
By Thomas Chambers (British Artist in New York)
Circa 1840
Source: National Gallery of Art

## Chapter VI

Despite my weariness from the long journey, I trembled with excitement and clung tightly to Uncle Karl's arm as our coach rumbled across the flat plains surrounding the ancient city of Leipzig. When my straining eyes finally caught sight of the gleaming tower of the Pleissenburg, the only remaining castle of three that the city possessed in the middle ages, I knew that we had only a short distance left to cover.

Passing through one of the seven narrow gates into the city was like entering a world unto itself, but almost at once I felt an atmosphere of strength, purposeful activity, and achievement. It enveloped me, overwhelmed me, and moved me to tears as I gazed upon the architecture of the city: houses, shops, printing establishments, warehouses, churches, university buildings, all were ranged in solid blocks up and down its narrow streets. There was a certain baroque elegance about its buildings, but they had an air somehow more utilitarian than picturesque, as if beneath the exterior one would find the plain, common sense solidity that embodied the Leipzig point of view.

This was the city that published more books than any other in the world; whose university had produced not only a Goethe, but generations of poets and savants; where for a quarter of a century as cantor of the Thomasschule, Johann Sebastian Bach had composed and produced his glorious choral works; whose famous Gewandhaus orchestra surpassed any other in Europe; where traders in goods of every imaginable sort had

Bauplatz für Felsches Café Français 1831 in Leipzig
Source: Public Domain Prints

converged three times a year since the twelfth century for the renowned Leipzig fairs. And all this without the patronage of a court and a ducal prince, as in many other German towns. Arts and letters were an integral part of life for bourgeois Leipzigers, and even in their cafes and taverns an aura of learning hung about them as they discussed and harangued on every subject. Whether it was in the Kaffeebaum on Fleischergasse or in "Auerbach's Cellar" of Goethe's *Faust*, an unsavory student haunt down a narrow lane, the conversation was intense, vibrant, and alive.

As we clattered over the cobblestones of the Neumarkt the city's daily life bustled all about us; there were few carriages, but an odd assortment of vehicles, from horse-drawn vats of wine on runners to two-wheeled carts groaning with newly published books, to the pushcarts of vendors hawking their wares. I caught my breath as we approached the Gewandhaus, or Clothier's Hall, so-called as if in defiance of all that was courtly elsewhere, a converted warehouse without portico, column, or approach to mark it as anything out of the ordinary. I begged Uncle Karl to let us stop for a moment so that I might see at once the famous hall from which poured forth so much glorious music. The door through which we entered was directly on the street; once inside we climbed a narrow staircase to reach a rather smaller than expected bare-walled space painted a frightful shade of yellow, with pew-like rows of seats at each side of the room facing each other and a platform at the end. Uncle Karl assured me that although it was anything but elegant, the acoustics were more than satisfactory, which I could hear for myself when the concert season opened in early October with the orchestra under the direction of its newly-appointed leader, Felix Mendelssohn.

Leipzig, I soon found, was in a state of excited anticipation over the arrival of the twenty-six year old Mendelssohn, already recognized as a master composer, pianist, organist, and conductor. The city's offer of the conductorship of the Gewandhaus orchestra was the highest appointment possible in Germany to a musician, so the anticipation was mutual. The musicians that he was to lead were highly professional, they were accustomed to the style of the classic masterpieces of Bach, Handel, Haydn, Mozart, and Beethoven, and audiences there expected more of their concerts than was the case elsewhere. With the convergence of these happy circumstances, the Gewandhaus orchestra under Mendelssohn was soon to become a model for all of Europe.

But for now, my immediate concern was to rest and prepare for my audition with Herr Wieck. The agreement between Father and this formidable pedagogue, all conducted through my Leipzig Uncle Hugo, was that if I was accepted as a pupil, I would board in his home so that I might take advantage of an atmosphere in which music was made, talked, and breathed almost every hour of every day. There had been a steady succession of student boarders in the commodious house at 579 Reichstrasse, so that was not at all an unusual arrangement. Uncle Karl called on Herr Wieck shortly after our arrival to set a date for my audition, and I settled into a routine of practicing five or six hours a day on the fine Rupp grand piano in Uncle Hugo's parlor.

The days passed quickly between practicing and walking about the city taking in the sights and sounds, with a visit or two to the A. Rupp & Sons factory where Uncle Hugo obviously delighted in showing me around. Occasionally my uncles and I walked out to Connewitz, a wooded area of Leipzig's surrounding plains, to escape the heat and congestion of the city. This pleasant excursion was usually followed by a leisurely supper at the Wasserschenke restaurant, a favorite gathering place for Leipzigers, then home to write letters to my family and to Herr Hoffman before retiring. I was calm and generally confident about my upcoming audition as Herr Hoffmann had prepared me so thoroughly, I felt, and I so much wanted the opportunity to study with the renowned Frederick Wieck.

On the appointed day Uncle Karl accompanied me to the Wiecks' house, where once inside the sounds of music emanating from seemingly every side filled me with awe. Frau Wieck was gracious in greeting me, then led me to a room with a grand piano to await her husband. She explained that Clara was practicing in another room of the house, Herr Wieck was giving a lesson in yet another, and one of her young sons was having a violin lesson in still another. Clara Wieck! I was listening to the already famous prodigy, the star in her father's crown, the living validation of his teaching methods. It was only at that moment that I felt my confidence wavering.

I regained my composure when Herr Wieck entered the room, a stern looking man, yet with an air about him that restored my confidence, as if he wanted my audition to be successful as much as I did. I took my place at the piano and began with a Beethoven sonata. All the years that Herr Hoffmann and I had worked seemed to come to fruition in the ensuing half hour and I felt that I had never played better. At the conclusion he told me that I was obviously gifted and well taught, that he would take me as a pupil, and that we would begin with the *Wohltemperirte Klavier* of Bach. I thanked him, then ran out of the room to find Uncle Karl before Herr Wieck noticed the tears beginning to roll down my cheeks.

In the next few weeks, as I settled into my new life, I often lay in my bed at night filled to overflowing with the joy of living in such a place, surrounded by such people. The Wieck household was pervaded with an atmosphere of application and accomplishment, as serious music making was the central focus of all its inhabitants. But it was not all work. Making music for the sheer pleasure of it was a regular feature as well. Almost every evening the most accomplished musicians of Leipzig would arrive at the door, instruments under their arms, ready and eager to try out the latest music coming from the presses of Breitkopf & Hartel.

Clara was unquestionably the center of interest at these musical evenings. She introduced the music of Frederic Chopin as soon as it appeared in print, as well as that of Robert Schumann, a frequent guest at these affairs, of Franz Schubert, and some of her own compositions. I had come to know her better during these weeks. Small and slender, with large, intense dark eyes, she constantly amazed me with the maturity and quiet grace of her mastery of the piano. She had debuted at the Gewandhaus at age eleven, had played for the great Goethe and crowned heads of Europe during tours with her father at age twelve, yet she remained refreshingly unspoiled by the adulation heaped upon her. Here I was at twenty, dazzled and inspired by the artistry of a girl not yet sixteen!

With the arrival in late August of Felix Mendelssohn to take up his duties as leader of the Gewandhaus orchestra, musical Leipzig reached a fever pitch. An aura of eminence and success hung about him; from his elegant, charming demeanor to the fervor of his music, he was instantly the object of general adoration. He brought with him a mode of orchestral conducting entirely new to Leipzig. Before, the first violinist rose now and then from his place to give a gesture to begin, or to indicate a choral entrance. Now for the first time, here was a conductor who used a baton, supervised the playing throughout, worked toward clean, concerted expressive musicianship. Mendelssohn was without doubt the idol of Leipzig.

Together with the cooler days of September came one memorable event after another. Distinguished musicians visiting the city increased in number as word of Mendelssohn's presence there spread throughout the musical world, with most of them paying a call at the Wiecks'. But Clara's sixteenth birthday on September 13 was one of the most memorable occasions of all. Mendelssohn and Schumann, together with a few other friends gathered at the Wiecks' at noon for a festive afternoon of eating, drinking champagne and opening of gifts by Clara. She rose to make the first formal speech of her life, holding her glass of champagne high in thanking her friends, then was called upon to play; she was followed by Mendelssohn who delighted us all with imitations of Liszt and Chopin at the piano.

The excitement of these days reached a new pitch with the visit, if only for a day, of Frederic Chopin. Now 25, he was

Clara Wieck, from an 1835 Lithograph
by Julius Giere (1807 – 1880)
Source: United States Library of Congress

returning to Paris where he was the raging idol, commanding enormous sums for playing or teaching, with each new composition snapped up as quickly as it appeared in the music shops. He and his friend Mendelssohn arrived at the Wiecks' on an afternoon not long after the birthday celebration, whereupon Clara played for him two of his Etudes and the last movement of his E minor Concerto. Chopin was lavish in his praise, then in return played one of his Nocturnes. I was very nearly overcome – by his elegant French manners, I suspect, as much as by his piano playing. But I was not the only one. Robert Schumann had already hailed Chopin as a genius in his magazine, the *Neue Zeitschrift fur Musik*, and his excitement, despite his usual quiet demeanor, was apparent – not to mention that of the curious Leipzigers who, hearing that Chopin was visiting at the Wiecks', had crept in to listen.

Yet another distinguished visitor during these heady days was Ignatz Moscheles from London. Clara charmed him by playing for him his G minor Concerto, followed by Clara, Mendelssohn, and Moscheles playing the Bach D minor Concerto for three keyboards, a triumphant discovery by Mendelssohn of an unpublished and practically unknown work of Bach's. Moscheles at once had this treasure copied to take back with him to London, and Mendelssohn scheduled it on one of his upcoming concerts, with himself, Clara, and Rakemann, a pianist of Bremen, as the performers.

The musical climax of this momentous autumn came in early November at the Gewandhaus when, with Mendelssohn conducting, Clara was soloist in the E minor Concerto of Chopin. I was dressed more elegantly than I had ever been in a blue velvet gown trimmed at the neck with silk roses, and Uncle Karl had never looked so distinguished as he did that night in his blue frock coat with velvet collar and little brass buttons. I took my place with the ladies in one of the rows of seats, while Uncle Karl, Uncle Hugo and the other men stood crowded around the wall behind us, as was the custom in the Gewandhaus.

Portrait of Felix Mendelssohn Bartholdy
by the English miniaturist
James Warren Childe (1778–1862),
painted in 1839 in London
Source: Public Domain

The program opened with a symphony of Haydn, then Clara, with her usual lack of affectation, seated herself at the piano and waited quietly for her entrance following the long, lovely orchestral theme beginning the Chopin concerto. This was the first time that I had heard the concerto in its entirety, with orchestral accompaniment, and I sat spellbound as Clara's fingers executed the difficulties of the first movement with sureness and exquisite beauty. But nothing had prepared me for the slow movement. The violins began with an almost plaintive quietness, then the orchestra virtually disappeared as the piano entered with a melody of such longing that I felt moved as I had never been before in my life. It was as if the music had touched some deep, unknown sadness within me, which puzzled me as I listened, for I had never known anything but love, security, and happiness. The feeling came over me suddenly and unexpectedly, just as it had when I bade farewell to my family and friends in New York only a few months before. But the sadness left me as quickly as it had come as the orchestra and piano began the third movement, a delightful *vivace* of Polish dance rhythms.

Clara's performance was rewarded with thunderous applause, and she and Mendelssohn were called again and again to the stage for bow after bow. An armful of flowers was presented to her as she smiled and acknowledged the cheers of the audience, gracefully sharing their adulation with the conductor and orchestra. Such a night I never expected to experience again, and when we all returned home after the concert, exhilarated and exhausted, I knew that I had to learn the Chopin E minor Concerto.

The next morning I was up early, quickly ate my breakfast as the first of the day's pupils was arriving, put on my cloak against the cold November air, and headed for the music shop. For the rest of the day I worked at the piano, going over and over the slow movement of the concerto until I had mastered it, as if driven by some unknown inner compulsion. That evening I played it for Herr Wieck who made some improvements

Portrait of Frédéric Chopin
By Maria Wodzińska, 1835
Source: Library of Congress

in my interpretation, then I fell into my bed with a comforting sense of accomplishment, drifting off into a deep sleep.

    A letter from Emilie arrived in the morning's post, and I went to my room to read it in privacy, as was my custom. The words stunned me and I sat down on the bed as I read that Mother was seriously ill again with pneumonia, that because her lungs were so weakened from the previous year's illness Dr. Darby feared that she could not survive the winter. I threw on my cloak and went immediately to Uncle Karl's with the letter. After he had finished reading it, I looked at him and in a barely audible voice said, "I must go home, Uncle Karl, I must see my mother."

The *Leipzig Gewandhaus with a Piece of Music*, the music is from Luigi Cherubini's "Ali Baba" (in Mendelssohn's hand).
The watercolor painting is for the album of Henriette Grabau, dated 1836.

## Chapter VII

I was grateful that our journey home had been relatively uneventful, given the time of year, but as our packet ship made its way through the Narrows, I was thinking how different my homecoming was from the joyous event I would have expected under other circumstances. The hope that I would find my mother alive had alternated daily with the fear that I was too late, keeping my emotions in turmoil but once into the comforting familiarity of the East River I watched the lights on shore flicker and glow against the dark sky and I felt a strange kind of serenity, a strength I had never known before. It was as if in that brief span of time I became fully grown, and I felt I was ready for whatever lay ahead.

Ships from everywhere were crowded along the piers and wharves, as always, but the docks seemed calm compared to the usual daytime clamor there. Steeples and domes were bathed in a kind of ethereal glow from the gaslights, and together with a light snow that was falling, gave the city something of a fairy tale aspect. Could the events of the past few months really have happened? Already they were beginning to seem like a dream. I could not possibly have experienced such things, could I?

As Uncle Karl and I waited with the other passengers to disembark, we could see that it was snowing harder now and we pulled our wraps closer around us to ward off the cold December night air. Once on shore I looked anxiously around for Father and Emilie, expecting that my hastily written letter telling them I was returning home had preceded me. They would be there with Asa and the carriage. Suddenly I saw Father coming toward us, and even in the dim light the moment I saw his face I knew we were too late. As I ran to him, his blue-gray eyes looked tired and his face was haggard, but his arms around me were strong and I knew he was glad to have us home again. Asa helped me into the carriage where Emilie was waiting, while Father and Uncle Karl went off to attend to the luggage. She told me quietly and without emotion that Mother had slipped peacefully away the first week of November. There had been a simple service at Trinity Church attended by many friends, but Father seemed unable as yet to deal with his grief, often sitting long hours before the fire in his study, lost in thought. She hoped that my being home and talking with him about my experiences of the past few months would help lift the mantle of gloom that had settled down about him.

The ride home seemed strangely peaceful, without tears, and presently Father asked about Uncle Hugo and said he wanted to hear all about Leipzig in the morning. When we reached the house I remembered how Emilie and I had run through the door not so long ago, laughing and crying, to tell Mother my exciting news, but this time when we entered I sensed a terrible emptiness as I looked about the familiar rooms. The atmosphere of warmth and serenity that my mother had created in our home was gone, seeming to leave only spaces and inhabitants.

Esther came to greet me, struggling to maintain her composure. Declining her offer to bring me something to eat, I walked into the parlor as if directed by some external power, sat down at the piano and began to play the slow movement of the Chopin E minor Concerto. That lovely plaintive music expressed for me, more profoundly than words or tears, the grief that overwhelmed me at that moment. I had not had time to memorize the notes, but my fingers moved surely and effortlessly over the keys until the end. I sat there for a moment, then suddenly feeling cold and weary I rose from the bench and walked up the stairs, eager for the warm comfort of my bed.

The next several days passed quietly, Father seeming more and more like himself, taking pleasure in my recounting the eventful months I had spent in his native home. Emilie confided to me that Father, while I was away, still talked of moving to Boston, and the two of us agreed that we should begin to think very seriously about the possibility. Perhaps this was the right time for such a change; our house could be sold at an enormous profit, and now that Mother was gone, Father could begin a new life there. We decided to wait before discussing it with him, however, continuing to turn the idea over in our own minds until he brought it up again.

December 16 dawned bleak and bitterly cold. Emilie and I remained inside the house, baking bread for supper and grateful for the warmth of the kitchen. Father arrived home at his usual time, changed into his warm smoking jacket and slippers, and settled down with the evening paper before the fire blazing in his study. By the time Esther called us to supper the wind had begun to howl, and looking out the front windows we could see the trees around the park being whipped about despite the heavy weight of their ice-coated branches. The gaslights along Broadway flickered on and off in the fierce wind, lending an eerie other-worldliness to the now deserted street. I shuddered as I pulled my shawl closer around me.

After supper Father retired to his study to read, I went to the piano to practice, and Emilie and Esther remained in the dining room discussing household matters. Suddenly, somewhere between eight and nine o'clock, the quietness of our domestic scene was shattered by the loud, sharp clanging of the dreaded fire alarm. Hurrying to the front windows, we saw that the signal atop City Hall indicated a location in the business and warehouse district of lower Manhattan. Father bolted up the stairs to change into his warmest clothing, and as he, now joined by Asa, ran out the front door a second alarm, frightening in its even sharper, more nervous tension, rang out. A third and fourth alarm followed in rapid succession.

Chopin First Piano Concerto in E Minor –
Orchestral Score from the Second Movement

Emilie and I ran upstairs to our room, and looking toward the southeast from our window seat could see jagged fingers of flames groping toward the sky, turning the darkness there into a glowing vivid red. A sickening fear crept over us with the realization that Father's factory and business, with the lodgings above now occupied by Uncle Karl, were located exactly in the area of the flames. We watched in shocked silence as men in silk hats and evening dress erupted from the Park Theatre, joining others in corduroy and work clothes, all running amidst the clanging fire engines and tolling bells toward the scene of the fire. It was obvious that this was a conflagration of terrifying proportions.

We remained frozen in the window seat as minutes then hours passed with no sign of Father, Uncle Karl or Asa. Fire engines from the upper part of the city continued to rush toward the scene, scattering throngs of excited citizens that had filled the streets, while the leaping flames and red glow spread farther and farther toward the south and east. Finally Emilie and I ran out into the street and could see that from Wall Street down the city was a burning cauldron, the flames fanned by the fierce northwest wind. We looked frantically about for someone who could have seen Father, finally spotting an exhausted and stunned fireman heading up Broadway. We asked him to come inside to warm himself before the fire, and introducing himself as Jack Boggs, he wearily accepted our offer.

While he gulped hot coffee and devoured the sausage and rolls that Esther brought, he recounted the last few nightmarish hours. The fire had originated in the store of Comstock & Adams in Merchant Street, a narrow street lined with tall wooden buildings occupied by dry goods and hardware merchants, all filled with stocks of immense value. The intense cold, with temperatures hovering below zero, was a primary cause of the rapid spread of the flames as the water was freezing in the hydrants and engines and hoses could be worked only with the greatest difficulty. Exhausted firemen were joined by citizens of every description in working the pumps or passing buckets of water along but the situation appeared hopeless as building after building toppled into the street and burning embers carried by the wind fell on buildings blocks away.

Mr. Boggs stopped talking for a moment and leaned his head against the back of Father's chair, closing his eyes as if to shut out the sight of it. As he sat forward again to down the last gulp of coffee, we inquired frantically about Father and his factory on Pearl Street. He said the fire had spread rapidly from Merchant Street to Hanover and Pearl Streets, leveling everything in its path, but he knew Father by sight, and once all hope was lost for his factory Father had joined in a futile effort to save the statue of Alexander Hamilton, newly erected in the rotunda of the Merchants Exchange on Wall Street. This splendid edifice, built only a few years before by public-spirited merchants and considered one of the showpieces of the city, was now a smoldering ruin, the front facade and magnificent marble columns all that remained. Just before the dome collapsed into the rotunda all the would-be rescuers had fled to safety, but he did not know of Father's whereabouts since then.

Rising from his chair, he thanked us, saying he needed to return to join volunteers in manning a boat to the Brooklyn Navy Yard, the purpose being to obtain explosives as there were none in the city. This was to be a dangerous mission in the face of the bitter wind and turbulent waters, but the only hope now to stop the fire was to blow up the buildings in its path. We wished him Godspeed as he left, then hurried upstairs to our bedroom window, anxiously scanning the crowd below for some sign of the men of our household. Finally just before dawn, we both cried out as we caught sight of Father walking slowly up Broadway, dazed and exhausted, his face and clothing blackened by dirt and soot. We ran downstairs and out into the street to meet him, calling for Esther to bring him something to eat.

His eyes looked strangely vacant as he sank into his chair and began slowly pulling off his boots and coat. While he sat staring into the fire he told us in a voice flat and emotionless,

A Barren Landscape 67

The Burning of the Merchants Exchange
By Nicolino V. Calyo
Source: United States Library of Congress

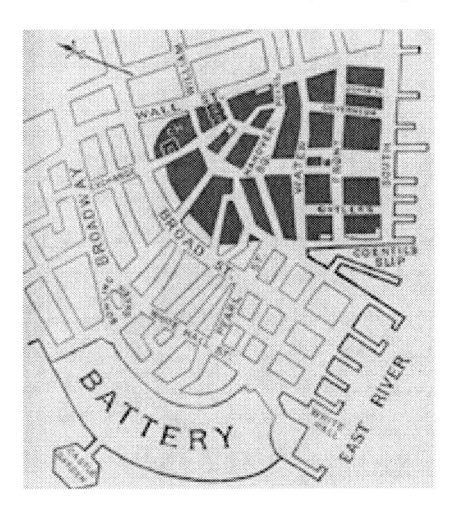

The Primary Affected Areas of The Great Fire –
Courtesy of City University of New York

as if someone we did not know were speaking, that the boat for Brooklyn had been launched, but it had not returned and he feared it was lost. If the explosives did not arrive soon only a miracle could save the city. He, Uncle Karl and Asa had tried to save what they could from the business, depositing box after box in what they believed to be a place of safety, but flames soon overtook it all, with the stocks of neighboring businesses as well. Nothing was saved. All the property between Wall Street and the river was destroyed, while to the west, everything east of Broadway was in ruins, including all the last traces of the old Dutch town.

At our urging, Father agreed to try to sleep before returning to the scene and let us help him up the stairs to his room, where he fell onto his bed fully clothed. Covering him with a warm wool blanket and closing his door softly behind us, we went to our own room to rest, still concerned over the whereabouts of Uncle Karl and Asa. In the dreary gray light of morning we could see from the window that the lower part of the city was hidden by a huge cloud of black smoke, while new fires were being kindled by burning timbers and embers blown about by the still raging northwest wind. Exhausted and fearful, we fell onto our beds and into fitful sleep.

We were awakened just after nine o'clock by a newsboy crying "Extra! Extra!" in the street below our window. Esther ran out to buy a copy of the *Courier* while we hurried downstairs to learn the latest news. We quickly scanned the front page, "There is no telling when the fire will be stopped; the hydrants are exhausted; the hoses of many of the engines are frozen and useless; the flames are extending; Wall Street from William to the East River totally destroyed; from 700 to 1,000 buildings are said to be gone." Within the hour a final edition appeared on the streets with the news that the fire was almost upon them and they were moving out, but not before reporting that supplies of gunpowder had arrived from the Navy Yard in Brooklyn and that "the sailors carried kegs and barrels of gunpowder amid a constant shower of fire as they followed their officers to the various buildings indicated for destruction." Thank God, Mr. Boggs!

Emilie and I dressed quickly and put the guest room in order for Uncle Karl, whose lodgings and personal belongings were now nothing more than a smoldering heap. As he and Asa had been without sleep for more than twenty-four hours, we expected them home at any moment. I tiptoed in to check on Father, to find that he had not moved from the position in which he had fallen onto his bed some hours before. Anger and despair welled up in me as I stood beside him watching him sleep, his blackened hands and face a silent testimony to his latest ordeal. How could any man withstand such devastating losses as he had suffered, in so short a space of time? Father was as strong as any man, but, God, *this*. . . tears had not come since I had been home and I struggled to hold them back now. At that moment I heard the front door open and anger was swept away by relief at the sound of Uncle Karl's voice.

Just behind him was Asa. Telling Esther to attend to him first, Emilie went into the kitchen for hot coffee while I helped the begrimed and unsteady man standing before me pull off his overcoat and gloves. Collapsing into Father's chair in the study, he told us that he and Asa had been helping spread gunpowder, but with the arrival of some 400 firemen from Philadelphia to relieve their exhausted and grateful brethren, they felt they could leave now that the situation seemed under control. He said looters had begun to move into the stricken area, but orders to shoot to kill should halt that unfortunate behavior shortly. Just as he appeared to be falling asleep in his chair, he got up, asked about Father, and upon being told he had been sleeping soundly for some hours now, nodded and shuffled up the stairs to the guest room, seemingly with barely enough strength left to close the door behind him.

The terrible sound of buildings exploding continued throughout that day and night and by morning the worst was over. But there was not an area of any other city in the world the destruction of which would involve a greater loss of capital or ruin the fortunes of a greater number of men. What had been the busiest and most important commercial section of the city was now a pile of smoldering rubble. Most of the great banks were gone, as were the Post-office and two churches. Next, many of the insurance companies were to be bankrupted by this disaster. The newspapers of December 18, 1835, reported the estimated loss at between fifteen and twenty million dollars; fifty acres containing twenty blocks of buildings and houses were destroyed.

Old New York was gone.

# Chapter VIII

The worst and the best year of my life closed quietly. As the New Year dawned, I sat in my window seat looking down at the snow-covered park below, a glistening, serene island surrounded by clattering streets, and I thought of all the peaceful hours I had spent there, without grief or care to weigh so heavily upon me. Emilie was still sleeping, the cries of the chimney sweep had long since faded into the distance, and the warm, sweet aroma from the kitchen soothed me as I pondered what the new year would bring.

Father had not yet emerged from the state of shock in which he had returned home that disastrous December morning, passing his days sitting at the window in his room staring blankly toward the southeast, neither speaking when spoken to nor acknowledging our presence when we entered the room. Asa attended to him with the tenderest care, adding logs to the blazing fire and arranging a warm throw over his legs against the chill seeping in around the window. Dr. Darby stopped by daily on his way home from the hospital, telling us in response to our anxious inquiries that time alone could heal Father's inner wounds and restore him to himself.

Uncle Karl remained with us, and as the days passed gradually assumed the role of head of the household. He, Emilie, and I held nightly discussions in Father's study, and before long a plan emerged whereby Uncle Karl would remain in New York to rebuild the business, living in the house until it was sold. Emilie and I would travel to Boston as soon as the weather improved to find a house there to accommodate our needs. Once moved, with Esther to help us put the house in order, Uncle Karl and Asa would bring Father.

In late February, at Dr. Darby's suggestion, I wrote to his son George, asking if he could be so kind as to locate a house or two for rent that Emilie and I might look at sometime during March. We would require two parlors, one for Emilie's schoolroom and one for my piano and the pupils I expected to teach there, a study for Father, and suitable quarters for Esther and Asa. In mid-March I received a reply that he had found a house on West Street near the Common that he thought might answer our needs perfectly. Emilie and I prepared at once to journey to Boston, writing first to George to thank him for his trouble and to give him the expected date of our arrival.

On a cold but clear and sunny afternoon in late March, Emilie and I alighted from the stagecoach at the Boston Stage house on Bromfield Street. Following George's directions, we walked north toward Tremont Street, which was considered the ceremonial area of Boston, having been the location from colonial days of the Royal Custom House, the King's Chapel, Royal Governor John Endicott's house and the Old Granary burial ground. Bromfield Street opened directly onto the burial ground on the opposite side of Tremont Street, and Emilie and I stopped for a moment to admire the carved granite gateway to the resting place of such illustrious early Bostonians as Paul Revere, Samuel Adams and Governor John Hancock. Turning west onto Tremont, we passed the Park Street Church, known as "brimstone corner" because of its zealous Congregational preachers, located next to the cemetery and on the site where once the town's grain was stored, hence the name given the burial ground. Across Park Street opened the vast park area known as the Boston Common, its elm and buttonwood trees waiting cautiously before sending forth their leafy heralds of spring, while children were laughing and playing beneath their bare branches.

Approaching St. Paul's Church, a dignified gray granite Greek temple with six Ionic columns, we could not resist a peek inside, which revealed an equally impressive interior. Just beyond St. Paul's, according to George's directions, was West Street, opening to Tremont and the Common on one end, to Washington Street the busy commercial center of Boston with its shops, inns, and taverns, on the other. Turning onto West Street we walked past several narrow, three storied red brick row houses standing flush with the sidewalk before stopping at one covered with ivy. The door was opened by a pleasant-looking woman who invited us inside and showed us around the light and spacious rooms overlooking a small brick-walled garden at the rear; I thought how lovely it must be in bloom. It was apparent to Emilie and me both that George was right – the house perfectly suited our needs.

Leaving a deposit with the owner, we hurried back to the stage house where a return coach to New York waited. Emilie was already seated inside and the driver had taken my arm to help me in when I heard a voice calling, "Miss Rupp! Miss Rupp!" I turned to see a breathless, slightly disheveled George Darby running toward me. "I'm so glad to have caught up with you, Miss Rupp! I had intended to meet you at the West Street house, but I was grading examinations and lost track of the time. I hope you found the house satisfactory." He looked so anxious that I couldn't help smiling a little as I replied, "Oh yes, Mr. Darby, it is perfect, and we are so very grateful to you for finding it. We expect to move shortly and once we are settled, Uncle Karl will bring Father and you must come to see him."

The driver was looking at his pocket watch, so I put out my hand to George and saw it virtually disappear into his; I remember thinking that he could reach a tenth on the piano with no trouble at all. With a promise to call on us as soon as we were settled, he left us to walk back across the Charles River Bridge to Cambridge. I watched him as the coach pulled away, then sat back and thought how pleasant it would be to have George coming to the house again after so many years, and how relieved I was that, because of him, we had found a suitable house with so little trouble. Now we could turn our attention to moving the furniture and other household goods, excepting what Father and Uncle Karl would require, before beginning a new life in a new and very different place. I found myself looking forward to it with anticipation – perhaps we could leave the pain of the past year behind us as well.

With the arrival of the first bright, fragrant days of May, with the last piece of furniture in place and the last cup washed and tucked into the cupboard, we were ready to welcome Father to his new home. Uncle Karl had written regularly of his progress, the latest news that he was now leaving his room for a daily walk with Asa the best that we had yet received, but this encouraging report was tempered with the addition that he still seemed lost in a world of his own, appearing to be oblivious to the city's life around him, yet still physically strong. It is only a matter of time, I told myself.

Esther had prepared his favorite dishes, and Emilie and I had filled his study with vases of flowers on the day of his expected arrival. His desk, his great leather chair by the fireplace, his books and prints were all arranged in his study as nearly as possible to the favorite room he was leaving behind. Once the remainder of his furniture arrived, we would arrange his bedchamber with comfortable familiarity as well. The back parlor was set up for Emilie's schoolroom, and in a corner of the front parlor stood my piano, with sofa, tables and chairs arranged as graciously as possible for guests as well as for pupils.

After spending the day checking and re-checking our preparations amid frequent trips to the front windows to watch for Father's carriage, at last in late afternoon clattering hooves stopped in front of our house. Running outside, we waited anxiously while Uncle Karl helped Father from the carriage before throwing our arms around him, hoping that he would return our joyous embrace. Was there the slightest glimmer of recognition when he turned his eyes toward us?

# A Barren Landscape

Detail of 1852 Map of Boston by J. Slatter,
showing West Street, Washington Street, and vicinity.
Published by Dripps, M. (Matthew). Source: Boston Public Library

Blinking to hold back the tears, we walked slowly with him into the house to his study, settling him into his great chair. His face looked tired and drawn, and he sat staring out the window while we talked of the things he would see and do now that he was in Boston.

As the last red streaks of sunset faded into twilight, it was apparent that he was weary from the journey; the faint glimmer that I thought I had detected on his arrival was gone and I wondered if I had only imagined it. Uncle Karl and Asa took him upstairs to his room, followed by Esther with his supper on a tray, while Emilie and I asked each other if that earlier brief hope was only an illusion. Were we merely deceiving ourselves, grasping at every tiny straw as a sign of recovery? Was one who had been so vitally alive destined to spend the rest of his days in that half-alive state? As I put out the lamps in the study, I swore to myself that never, ever again would I consider that possibility.

Our first caller arrived the next afternoon, as he had promised. George sat in Father's study and told him about his two years of travel in Europe after his graduation from Columbia; about his position as instructor in modern languages at Harvard; about his having had a half-dozen or so short stories published in one or another of the literary magazines; about a novel that was taking shape in his mind. Father sat with his gaze fixed upon George as he talked, and although there was no discernible sign that he was listening, I thought I detected once again the slightest hint of light in those once all-encompassing eyes.

As I showed George to the door after his brief first visit with Father, he looked at me with the same serious expression that I remembered from my childhood. "Miss Rupp, I will come often if I may, and read some of my writings to your father, the way I did while I was in college. I will ask his opinion, as I did then, and perhaps at some point, he will respond. It is worth a try, don't you agree?" I replied that my sister and I would be most grateful for any time that he felt he could spare from his duties, and once again seeing my hand disappear into his, I bade him goodbye.

At first George came twice weekly, then three times, never staying more than half an hour, reading first his published stories as he felt they were the best things he had done, asking questions that went unanswered. But as the weeks passed, George began to tell Emilie and me that he was becoming more and more certain that Father was listening, that it was only a matter of time before he would respond. Father loved literature above all else, and if there were any way to reach him, I knew this had to be the way. Each time I said goodbye to George at the door I thanked him again and again, telling him that when Father did recover the credit would be his alone. And each time he only looked at me with that serious expression and squeezed my hand a little before turning to leave.

One early summer afternoon as Emilie and I strolled with Father in the garden behind the house, enjoying the exuberant beauty of the rhododendrons and the birds chattering in the still branches above our heads, we were suddenly stopped short in our steps by the sound of Father's voice asking, "Is George coming today?" Emilie and I stared at each other in astonishment. Had Father really spoken to us or were our ears playing tricks? "Yes, Father", Emilie answered, her voice trembling, "he should be here at any moment now, so we should go back inside before he arrives."

When George left Father that afternoon, Emilie and I were waiting for him in the front hall, but we knew as soon as he closed the study doors behind him that something momentous had taken place. His dark eyes shone and he smiled almost shyly as he took both our hands in his and told us that he and Father had just finished a most interesting discussion of his ideas for the proposed novel. Emilie rushed off to the study while George and I just stood there looking at each other, as if there were no words adequate to express our feelings at that moment. Almost unconsciously, I put my hand out to him as I always had done before and we stood there looking at each other, oblivious of my outstretched hand. Then, without warning, I felt his arms around me and mine were around him and we held each other so tightly that I could scarcely get my breath. After a moment he let me go and, without a word, turned and walked out the door.

The National Lancers with the Reviewing Officers on the Boston Common
1837
By: Charles Hubbard, American, 1801–1876
Lithograph, hand-colored.
Source: Museum of Fine Arts, Boston.

# Chapter IX

Whereas a relentless hunger for wealth characterized New York City, a relentless thirst for knowledge characterized Boston. Small, isolated, and homogeneous, it nevertheless felt that it was destined to lead America toward a glorious future. Had not New England played a major role in two victorious wars with England? Had not its shipping and factories - located in every village with a waterfall - provided the wealth with which to achieve this destiny? Knowledge was the way to the golden age. Was that not the gospel their Unitarian ministers, learned and cultivated men, ceaselessly preached? One who was to leave the ministry to find his own destiny in the village of Concord said it plainly: "I do not speak with any fondness, but the language of coldest history when I say that Boston commands attention as the town which was appointed in the destiny of nations to lead the civilization of North America." Boston may have been small and provincial, but it had a mission.

The older patrician families equated wealth with responsibility; they possessed an inherent respect for learning, a regard for manners and decorum, scrupulousness in all things, and in all things, pride. Had not the minister Joseph Buckminster preached to the young men of Harvard College that they were "destined to witness the dawn of our Augustan age and to contribute to its glory?" Had not the young men responded by building churches, parks and public buildings, schools, asylums and hospitals along with their mansions? Had they not looked upon Harvard College, the wellspring of the village of Cambridge across the Charles, as their personal responsibility, founding chairs that bore their names, sending their own sons there as a matter of course?

Had they not founded the first literary magazine, the *North American Review* that could hold its own with the finest reviews of the world? With the publication of Bryant's "Thanatopsis" it had given notice that America was ready for native writers and poets. Its editors were aware of all the important writers in England, France, and Germany, but they had published the work of Cooper, Irving and Bryant as their equals, providing an outlet for them and the other American writers who were appearing on every hand. And the establishment of the Handel and Haydn Society to present great choral works pointed the way for music as the *North American Review* pointed the way in letters.

Though Boston had little general interest in art in those days, they did cherish their portrait painters. It was pride – family pride, wealth, public spirit that kept the portrait painters busy. Foremost among these was Gilbert Stuart, who had studied in Europe and whose skill perpetuated the likenesses and accomplishments of the patricians on canvas. And there was the Boston Athenaeum, founded in 1807 by Joseph Buckminster with his personal library of 3,000 volumes, to which had been added the great collection of books belonging to John Quincy Adams. On any day scholars could be seen sitting at their tables in one of the alcoves, books and papers spread about them. In addition, there were a number of extensive private libraries which were generally available to students and scholars. There was a certain amount of rivalry for the distinction of owning the finest library in Boston, in some cases the collection of books literally filling the house from attic to cellar.

In the midst of all this intellectual ferment, or rather because of it, Boston furnished a ready and eager audience for the rapidly spreading lyceum system. Educated men readily accepted lecturing as their contribution to public education.

At least five different organizations on almost every evening of the week offered public courses to which Bostonians flocked by the thousands; lecturers were noted personages from the literary, scientific, educational, ecclesiastical and political worlds. Ticket prices were low, usually two dollars for a series of lectures, but enough to enable sponsors to pay an honorarium, something entirely new, to the speakers.

Not only in Boston, but all over New England, there was a passionate interest in education and self- improvement. In every village one could find courses offered in chemistry, botany, history, literature, and philosophy, with crowds of workmen on winter nights listening with rapt attention. Though Harvard set the pace for learning for the well-to-do, the passion had spread through all the other strata of society as well. If it was not unique for a young man at his graduation from Harvard to read French, Italian, Spanish, Latin, and Greek, there were also some like the "learned blacksmith" of Worcester, who had learned Greek while an apprentice and in the evenings, after a full day's work, mastered forty other languages. Or there were the factory girls of Lowell. They wrote poetry, studied German, and could discuss Wordsworth, Coleridge and Macaulay. Many of these girls went West as schoolteachers, founding "improvement circles" on the Illinois and Wisconsin prairies.

One of the lecturers in Boston and its environs of Cambridge and Concord at this time was a tall, thin young man named Ralph Waldo Emerson. He belonged to one of Boston's oldest scholarly families, but he had drifted in and out of Harvard before drifting in and out of the ministry and school teaching. In 1834 he had settled in the village of Concord, where he found in the solitude of the woods and fields a language by which to give expression to his own thoughts; he was a thinker, looking into himself to reveal the powers that dwelled within the soul of every man. The Cambridge theologians thought him a pantheist and a German mystic; others were less kind; they called his ideas "conceited, laborious nonsense."

But Bostonians flocked to his lectures, and before long he

American Philosopher/Poet Ralph Waldo Emerson
Dated 1859
Source: United States Library of Congress

began to attract a considerable following, especially among the younger people. The effect of his essays and lectures on them was like a trumpet call, heralding the authority of their own unconscious natures, summoning them to new and noble endeavors. One might not always understand what he was saying, but he said it so beautifully; of course, there were those who thought HE did not always understand what he was saying. Newly arrived Professor Henry Wadsworth Longfellow wrote to a friend:

> Don't fail to hear Emerson's lectures. The difference between him and most other lecturers is this: from Emerson you go away and remember nothing, save that you have been much delighted; you have had a pleasant dream in which angelic voices spake. From most other lecturers you go away and remember nothing, save that you have been lamentably *bored*, you have had the *nightmare*, and have heard her colt neigh."

In the spring of 1836, while we were settling into Boston, Emerson began to meet with a few like-minded friends to discuss the ideas of the German and French philosophers. They called themselves Transcendentalists, and Emerson's little book entitled *Nature* became their textbook. John Quincy Adams explained the origin of Transcendentalism in this way: "A young man named Ralph Waldo Emerson, after failing in the everyday occupations of Unitarian minister and school master, starts a new doctrine of Transcendentalism, declares all the old revelations superannuated and worn out, and announces the approach of new revelations and prophecies." Nevertheless, the doctrine of the supremacy of the individual, his original and unique quality, his acting in harmony with his own nature, had a great effect on those given to introspection, and they drank it in as if possessed of an unquenchable thirst.

George Darby's regular visits continued and Father, though now past fifty, seemed reborn, reading and discussing George's work with him while forming a plan in his own mind to translate certain works of Goethe, who had died in 1832. Boston might have looked askance at the great German writer's morals, but there was no denying his genius and who better than a German American to undertake the task? Boston was alive with activities outside the walls of Father's study, however, and one by one they began to engage his interest.

George had introduced him to James Fields' Old Corner Bookstore on Washington Street, where he could browse at pleasure; he could attend a reading of Shakespeare by Fanny Kemble, a Sunday evening Handel and Haydn Society concert or a performance by Edwin Booth at the Tremont Theatre; he could view Stuart's portraits of George and Martha Washington or a collection of paintings by Washington Allston at the Athenaeum. Often he and George walked across the bridge to Cambridge to hear a lecture by Emerson, Daniel Webster or Oliver Wendell Holmes. George had introduced Father as well to the gentle, white-haired Allston, painter and man of letters who, after years in Europe, had settled at Cambridgeport, midway between Boston and Cambridge. Charming, gracious, and refined, Allston entertained a steady stream of visitors to his painting room with its great north window, dusty floor and smell of stale cigar smoke.

But somehow something had gone sadly awry with this American Titian. Upon his graduation from Harvard in 1800 he had left for Europe full of hopes to produce masterpieces in the tradition of the great Venetians, and by the time he returned to Boston in 1818 he had achieved an admirable reputation. He had begun the vast painting that was to be the crowning achievement of his career, but instead became the nightmare of his life, "Belshazzar's Feast." Now a legendary figure as he grew older, he still struggled to finish the unfinishable picture, his face a study in unrealized expectations. His great talent seemed to have dried up, "stunted on the scant soil and withered by the cold winds of that fearful Cambridgeport," according to the American sculptor W. W. Story, who found

Gilbert Stuart Portrait of George Washington
at Dorchester Heights, 1806
Source: The Boston Museum of Fine Art

Rome as congenial to his art as Allston had years earlier. Father enjoyed nothing better than a conversation with this amiable man over a glass of wine and a good cigar.

Meanwhile, Emilie had begun teaching a class of fifteen young girls in the back parlor, instructing not only in arithmetic, geography and spelling, but in drawing and music as well. The girls trooped to the front parlor three times a week to sing from songbooks of Emilie's choosing, while I accompanied on the piano. They seemed to thrive in the relaxed, cheerful atmosphere of Emilie's schoolroom, with light streaming in at the windows, pictures on the walls, a vase of flowers on her desk. As for me, I had enrolled ten pupils of my own, my study with Frederick Wieck in Leipzig the drawing card I had expected it to be. In addition, I was scheduled for a recital in Chickering's rooms on Tremont Street some weeks hence for which I was preparing thoroughly, despite the fact that these concerts, though well attended, were played to a rather undiscriminating audience. But then, I saw that as my mission – to raise the standard of musical appreciation by playing works of the greatest composers well.

George and I were spending more time together, attending concerts and lectures as the winter wore on. I confessed to him how much I missed the rich musical activity of Leipzig with its symphony concerts and distinguished musicians; Boston had formed a Philharmonic Orchestra some years earlier, but it had failed and no other had taken its place. He understood and sympathized, and I sensed that here was someone I could confide my hopes and disappointments to, thoughts and feelings I could not share with anyone before, always having resolved such matters for myself in the quiet solitude of my window seat. Then I listened as he told me of the rewards and frustrations of teaching students who sometimes seemed uninterested or inattentive, while at the same time trying to produce literary works of his own.

The bulk of the instruction in modern languages at Harvard was given by instructors like George, while the professors such as Henry Longfellow lectured on European literature of the past two or three centuries, his current series on Dante an example. Something of a dandy in his dress, no doubt the influence of his years in Europe, he sat with his students around a table in University Hall, discoursing in soft, lyrical tones on Anglo-Saxon bards, French Trouveres and Frankish legends. As in his college oration years before, he urged his young students to create a national literature from native materials, an admonition expressed poetically some time later when his fame had spread throughout the land:

> O thou sculptor, painter, poet!
> Take this lesson to thy heart:
> That is best which lieth nearest;
> Shape from that thy work of art

## Chapter X

Near the center of Boston Common stood an ancient tree known to all thereabouts as the Old Elm, revered by generations of Bostonians for its majesty and beauty. It had provided shade and shelter to generations of cows, as well, for as far back as anyone could remember, until an order passed in 1830 banished the four-legged tenants from their green pasture and shady retreat. The Old Elm had withstood the storms and gales of centuries, witnessing beneath its mighty branches the ongoing saga of the human race. What a history it could tell!

It was there, one early summer evening in 1837, beneath the rustling leaves of that great tree that George Darby asked me to be his wife. We were walking back to West Street after a Sunday afternoon musicale at the Appletons' Beacon Street mansion across the Common, where I had played Schubert, Schumann, and Chopin to a most receptive audience. I felt the same kind of exhilaration I always felt when a concert had gone well, but then, I thought, the champagne at the reception afterward might have had something to do with it, too. Or perhaps it was having George beside me to share in the glow of a good performance, smiling at me with those dark eyes so full of love.

I suppose I had known for a long time that I wanted to share the rest of my life with George, but I wasn't sure before now of his feelings. His life seemed so filled with teaching and writing that I wondered whether there was any room left in it for

The Old Elm on Boston Common
Circa 1845
Source: Library of Congress

marriage. But there was no doubt now as he stood looking at me so earnestly, and before I could finish murmuring "yes, yes, yes," his arms were around me again for the first time since that day in the front hall and I felt a happiness more complete than any I had ever known. He told me, then, that we would have to wait for a year or so until he could earn enough from writing to supplement his instructor's salary, meager as it was, but I would have waited an eternity. Besides, I thought, that would give me more time to establish myself as a concert artist before taking on the responsibilities of a household and the likelihood of children.

We decided George should ask Father's permission that very evening, which I knew was a mere formality, as Father already thought of him as a son. How pleased he would be to give his consent! We hurried across Tremont Street, oblivious to the traffic and humanity around us, as if our newly professed love set us apart from all other mortals with their dull and ordinary concerns. Then I thought of poor Henry Longfellow, so unhappy in his unrequited love for Fanny Appleton; he scarcely took his eyes off her during the entire evening, and I thought how strange that love could make one so happy or so miserable.

On reaching the West Street house, George went directly to Father's study, while I ran upstairs to find Emilie. She was at her desk preparing lessons when I burst into the room with my news. We sat on her bed and laughed and cried and hugged and talked as we had on so many happy occasions before. Then the seriousness of the course I had embarked upon began to dawn on us and our talk became quieter, before we heard Father calling to us from the bottom of the stairs, "Eliza, Emilie! This calls for a celebration!," while Asa and Esther hurried off to fetch a bottle of Father's finest champagne and the elegant crystal glasses.

The weeks passed quickly as I eagerly anticipated every visit from George, every long walk we took together while talking over our hopes and plans for the future. Often our sojourns took us across the bridge to Cambridge, where we strolled through

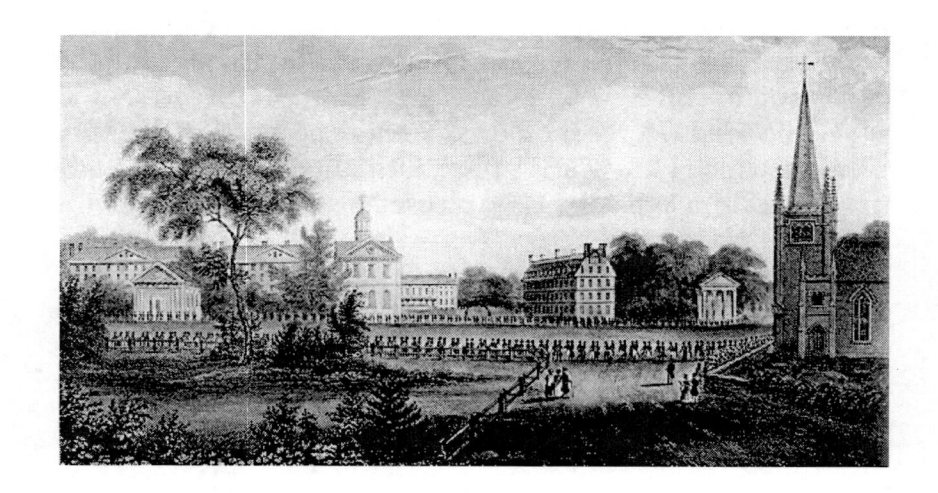

Harvard University Alumni Procession, 1836
By Eliza Susan Quincy

Harvard Yard with its solid buildings clustered around fields of green, thence to Brattle Street past the fine old mansion known as Craigie House where Longfellow had lately taken rooms. This stately residence had been built before the Revolution and had served as Washington's headquarters during the siege of Boston, but in falling upon lean times had been turned into an elegant boarding house. Longfellow's spacious rooms looked out over the Charles River to the Brighton meadows beyond and life there, with its comfortable furnishings, well-stocked cellar, and solicitous servants, suited Longfellow perfectly. He could never have dreamt in that summer of 1837 that it was to be his home for life, for in some few years he was to win his beloved Fanny, and Craigie House was a wedding gift to them from her wealthy father.

Longfellow by now had already achieved a measure of literary recognition with his published poems and a book, *Outre-Mer*, and before long he exchanged his colorful garb for a professorial black frock coat as he lectured to his students with imagination and enthusiasm over the whole range of European literature. Scholar and man of letters, no one before him had brought so great a scope of literary culture to the classroom.

Nathaniel Hawthorne, whom Longfellow had not seen since their college days at Bowdoin, had read *Outre-Mer*, and from his "owl's nest" in Salem, with some trepidation, sent Longfellow a gracious letter and a copy of his own first published book, *Twice Told Tales*.

> Since we last met which I remember was in Sawtelle's room, when you read a farewell poem to the class - ever since that time, I have secluded myself from society. And yet I never meant such a thing, nor dreamed what sort of life I was going to lead. . . I have seen so little of the world that I have nothing but thin air to concoct my stories of; and it is not easy to give a life-like semblance to such shadowy stuff.

Portrait of Nathaniel Hawthorne
by Charles Osgood (1809 to 1890), painted in 1840
Source: Peabody Essex Museum

Although not asked to do so, Longfellow, after finishing the book, sat down at once and wrote a glowing review of *Twice Told Tales* for the *North American Review*, still the authoritarian periodical of literary criticism. In gratitude, Hawthorne travelled to Cambridge to see him, beginning a life-long, though not close, friendship, meeting from time to time to share dinner, a bottle of wine and a long conversation.

These two men, each of whom was to earn such eminence in letters, could not have differed more in the roads they took toward their separate destinies. Longfellow, though still under thirty, had already achieved distinction in academic life; his father was a prominent lawyer in the state; Bowdoin had paid his expenses for two years of travel in Europe to make himself proficient before returning to occupy the chair of modern languages there. He was twenty-six when he received a letter from Josiah Quincy, President of Harvard, offering him their modern languages chair, with the stipulation that he must first spend another year in Europe to strengthen his German. In 1837 he took up his duties at Harvard, to remain there until 1854 when, famous and revered, he retired to devote himself exclusively to his writing.

Hawthorne's father was a sea captain who died in a foreign port when the boy was four, whereupon his mother shut herself in her chamber from which she rarely emerged for as long as she lived. Two sisters, both of whom adored him, became recluses as well, so it was not surprising that Hawthorne, returning home to Salem after college, retreated to his attic room, picked up his pen, and began to write the tales that his rich and vivid, if brooding, imagination suggested to him. But despite the differences in background and temperament between them, Longfellow and Hawthorne came to respect one another as writers and as men. Though success and wealth came early to Longfellow, Hawthorne struggled against poverty until well into middle age; but in one respect they were alike - both were to know idyllic marriages to accomplished women.

Emerson's lectures in Cambridge, meanwhile, were

becoming social as well as intellectual events not to be missed. Father, Emilie, George and I were in the audience in August 1837, when he delivered the Phi Beta Kappa address at Harvard on "The American Scholar", churning the smug and placid academic waters of Cambridge with gale force. He began benignly enough, but then as his audience sat in stony silence he told them that books were for a scholar's idle times; the scholar should learn from his own experience and from nature, "whose laws are the laws of his own mind." But the shock of this address paled beside one delivered to the Harvard Divinity School a year later.

This time he challenged religious rather than scholarly tradition. He admonished the young men who were about to be ordained, "Go alone, refuse good models, even those which are sacred in the imagination of men, and cast behind you all conformity. Do not be afraid of degrading the character of Jesus by representing him as a man. To do so is to indicate with sufficient clearness the falsity of our theology." Then he retreated to the calm refuge of Concord while the storm he had stirred up in Unitarian Cambridge raged on.

George continued to write short stories for publication in various periodicals during this year, but unfortunately he was rarely paid for his work. The reading public could not support the number of literary magazines that were sprouting up on every side so that many disappeared as quickly as they had come. Most blamed the financial panic of 1837 for their straits, but for whatever reason, George was not able to earn the extra income from his writing that he had hoped for, thus the year we had expected to wait for our marriage had now turned into two. He would not allow the small income I was earning from teaching and playing to be factored in as he said it could not be counted on once we were married. And he was too proud to accept financial support from Father, whose resources had been considerably diminished, at any rate, by the disastrous fire that destroyed his business.

In 1839 a poem written by Longfellow entitled "Psalm of Life" appeared in a New York periodical, the *Knickerbocker*, and almost overnight became the most quoted, discussed and eulogized poem ever published. Editors in Boston, New York, and Philadelphia scrambled to solicit contributions from him. After a few months he collected several of his poems into a book under the title *Voices of the Night*:

> I heard the trailing garments of the Night
>    Sweep through her marble halls!
> I saw her sable skirts all fringed with light
>    From the celestial walls!

The astonishing success of this slim volume exceeded Longfellow's most optimistic hopes. Within a month the first edition of 900 copies was sold out and within a year the book had gone into its fourth printing. A literary critic in the *North American Review* wrote that the new poems in *Voices of the Night* "are among the most remarkable poetical compositions which have ever appeared in the United States." "Nothing equal to some of them," Hawthorne wrote to Longfellow, "was ever written in this world - this western world, I mean, and it would not hurt my conscience much to include the other hemisphere." During the few years that followed, the growth of Longfellow's reputation as a poet was to be rapid and phenomenal. The "eminence in literature" of which he had spoken in his Bowdoin oration was to be his own in full measure.

## Chapter XI

The year 1840 ushered in a decade of unprecedented intellectual and cultural activity in Boston. The air fairly crackled with reform - education, abolition, temperance, women's rights - accompanied by a new focus on music and art. Prosperity and confidence began to return, too, as the depression years following the Panic of 1837 waned.

George's fortunes had improved as well. He felt he was now earning enough additional income from his writing that we could be married and, at last, the date was set for late summer. I was preparing two or three recitals to which I had committed and wished to fulfill before my marriage; I wanted to be nothing more than George Darby's wife for the first few months. George had begun work on his novel, a story laid in the Dutch period of America's history. Much of his free time was spent in the Athenaeum researching those early years, or in reading documents and papers handed down through generations of his mother's Dutch family whose vast upper Hudson Valley land holdings, because of her parents' sympathies toward the Crown, were confiscated after the Revolution. Thus occupied, we knew that after our long wait these last weeks would pass quickly.

In the meantime, a new family had moved into the house next door, the three daughters all destined to play major roles in America's cultural development, though it was to be, for two of them, by marriage. The Peabodys had come from Salem where Dr. Peabody practiced homeopathic medicine and Mrs. Peabody kept school whenever the family's financial straits required it, which was most of the time. Dr. Peabody opened a homeopathic drug shop in a front corner room of the house while Mrs. Peabody and the eldest daughter, Elizabeth, set about having shelves built along the walls of the front parlor, intending to turn it into a bookshop and lending library of modern foreign literature.

Elizabeth, now in her early thirties, was well known in Boston intellectual circles as the indomitable friend of all good causes, but recently she had acquired a measure of notoriety as teaching assistant to Bronson Alcott in his controversial Temple School. After the failure of the school she turned the full force of her considerable energy and enthusiasm into this newest venture, which included publishing children's books, among them Hawthorne's *Grandfather's Chair*, on a creaking, groaning printing press stationed in a little back room. Through Elizabeth's friendship with Emerson, the bookshop before long became a rendezvous for the Transcendentalists.

Besides Emerson and his Concord apostle and fellow poet Henry Thoreau, who made occasional trips to Boston, other frequenters of the bookshop, for reasons other than to discuss philosophy, were Hawthorne who was engaged to the youngest daughter, Sophia; Horace Mann, educational reformer instrumental in founding the State Board of Education who came, with hands full of papers covered with figures and data, to see Mary; and Washington Allston, who suggested that Elizabeth sell art supplies, arranging for her to become sole New England agent for a London firm. Then there was the group of twenty-five ladies who came every Wednesday morning at eleven for Margaret Fuller's "conversations," a series of lectures by a woman known for her satire and her scholarship. Given the same thorough classical education that her brothers received there was no question of her intellectual attainments; she had acquired an air of pompous intellectual vanity as well.

But ladies of various ages came from Cambridge, from

Engraving of Margaret Fuller
(Sarah Margaret Fuller Ossoli)
Source: Library of Congress

country homes in Brookline, and from nearby Beacon Street to willingly subject themselves to Margaret Fuller's contemptuous attitude toward those less learned than she. Her aims were admirable enough: "to pass in review the departments of thought and knowledge, and endeavor to place them in due relation to one another in our minds. To systematize thought, and give a precision and clearness in which our sex are deficient . . . to ascertain how we may make best use of our means for building up the life of thought upon the life of action." Some of her "conversations," more often monologues, were on the subject of Greek mythology, some on the fine arts, but when she swept into the West Street bookroom precisely as the bells of St. Paul's sounded eleven o'clock each Wednesday, twenty-five earnest Boston ladies were certain they were to leave a good deal more enlightened than when they had arrived.

Emilie and I soon became acquainted with the Peabody sisters and were invited by Elizabeth to attend a "conversation." She graciously introduced us to the ladies as they assembled, then we took our seats with the rest to await Miss Fuller's entrance. The subject on that particular morning was "the Sphinx." She began, "Like the Greeks we still have our unanswered riddles; like the Egyptians we still have our Sphinx. Ladies, what is the Sphinx?" Miss Fuller raised her forefinger and looked enquiringly around the room. After one or two hesitant responses from the audience, someone called out, "Tell us your definition of the Sphinx."

Squinting her eyes as they swept over us, she replied:

> To me it represents the development of a thought, founding itself upon the animal until it grows upward into calm, placid power. I revere our good ancients who did not throw away any of the gifts of God, who were neither materialists nor immaterialists, but who made matter always subservient to the highest ends of the Spirit. Matter, like the past, is a curtain upon which

we must embroider the Spirit. Matter, like God, is the background against which our souls are thrown. To me this interrelation solves the mystery of man, the riddle of the Sphinx.

I thought to myself, well, the mystery of the Sphinx has finally been solved - and all in one morning. I had understood almost nothing of what she had said, but I suspected the earnest Boston ladies were no better off in this respect than I.

I declined subsequent invitations to Margaret Fuller's "conversations," but Emilie found a certain fascination in them and paid to hear the entire series. I preferred to visit the bookstore when one or another of the literary personages was present, especially the reserved and darkly handsome Hawthorne, in whom I sensed a kindred spirit, if only in that neither of us was particularly in sympathy with the mystical musings and incessant talk of the Transcendentalists. I also sensed that he endured the self-conscious culture of 13 West Street only for the sake of a daughter of the house, his beloved Sophia. In the back room Elizabeth published, along with the children's books, the quarterly of Transcendentalism, the *Dial*, edited by Margaret Fuller and intended to spread their ideas to a larger audience than their own circle, but it was too limited in appeal and was destined to be short-lived.

Of the visitors to 13 West Street, the one who interested me most was Mr. Thoreau. He was Emerson's natural, self-reliant man personified; he represented the practical application of Emerson's ideas. Thoreau, like Hawthorne, was impatient with ideas that had no connection with life; he believed that one's life should illustrate one's beliefs. Whereas Emerson thought of nature in abstractions, Thoreau was nature itself, on intimate terms with all the animals and with every growing thing in and around Concord. And while Emerson lived a comfortable life in Concord with wife, children, servants, and continual visitors as he expounded his doctrine of nonconformity and self-reliance, Thoreau wished nothing more

Horace Mann Daguerreotype by Southworth & Hawes
Circa 1850
Source: The Metropolitan Museum of Art

than to make himself independent of society, desiring above all things the freedom to study, to observe nature and to write. To gain this freedom he was willing to deny himself most of the possessions which other people labored incessantly to acquire. "The life which men praise and regard as successful is but one kind. " No wonder Hawthorne found him "a healthy and wholesome man to know."

The Peabody daughter with whom Emilie was most in sympathy was Mary. Possessed of a quiet grace and refined features, she was in love with Horace Mann. Tall, prematurely gray, and single-minded as he hustled about in his long black frock coat, Mr. Mann had given up a promising career in law and politics in 1837 to accept the Secretaryship of the newly founded State Board of Education. He immediately threw himself into a tour of towns and villages of the state, collecting facts and figures about the public schools, accepting every invitation to lecture on the lyceum circuit about his passion, education for the people. The information thus gathered he edited into the first of his bimonthly school reports, *The Common School Journal.* Reform-minded Boston was roused to the importance of education and he realized that he must lay the foundation for an entire public school system while public interest was at its height. "None of you is so high as not to need the education of the people as a safeguard; none of you is so low as to be beneath its lifting power." On the occasions that he vigorously replied to his critics in the *Journal* it often became the most discussed publication in Boston.

In addition to the school reports, *The Common School Journal* featured lessons in geography, drawing, or spelling, most often written by Mary Peabody and accompanied by her delicate ink drawings of cubes and cones. She was at work as well on a geography to be published in installments in the *Journal,* for which she received no pay beyond what she considered the privilege of working with her dear Mr. Mann. Many a late night she spent helping him sort out information for his school reports or for questionnaires to be sent to schools around the state, afterwards organizing and tabulating the replies. But her patient and selfless devotion would be rewarded when in 1843 she would become his wife and share for life the remarkable career that was to make him internationally known as the founder of the American public school system.

The honor of delivering the Fourth of July oration, usually bestowed on Boston's favorite orators Daniel Webster, Edward Everett or Josiah Quincy, was Horace Mann's this year and he looked forward to it with no small measure of anxiety. "I find that expectations in some quarters are raised high and it will be difficult to satisfy them." On the morning of the great celebration the air was filled with patriotic enthusiasm. Bunting and flags were hung from houses and shops and cannon boomed from ships in the harbor. Gaily-painted wheelbarrows offered refreshments to celebrants around the Common, while schoolchildren marched about carrying flower wreaths in memory of the heroes of the Revolution.

In front of City Hall at half past ten Mann took his place in the procession to the dais from which he was to deliver his address with fervor and conviction. In an impassioned climax to his long oration, he implored his audience:

> Pour out light and truth, as God pours sunshine and rain. No longer seek knowledge as the luxury of the few, but dispense it amongst all as the bread of life. Learn only how ignorant may learn; how the innocent may be preserved; the vicious reclaimed...collect whatever of talent, erudition or eloquence, or authority, the broad land can supply, and go forth, and TEACH THIS PEOPLE.

As he stepped to his seat, wiping away the perspiration pouring from his face, the audience sat first in immobile silence, then erupted in tumultuous applause, bringing him to his feet again and again to acknowledge their acclaim.

As we walked home to West Street afterwards Emilie was

quiet and thoughtful while Father, George, and I discussed the oration and the effect it had had on the audience. The real verdict came in August, however, when "seventeen thousand copies of my oration have been published and another edition of ten thousand is to be published this week." By then I knew that Emilie had found her great and noble cause.

## Chapter XII

With the Education Act of 1789 Boston had laid the foundation of the first comprehensive public school system in America. The Act organized the loose system of schools already existing and, for the first time, provided for the schooling of girls at public expense, called for revisions and uniformity in the curricula, and formed a permanent school committee. By the early nineteenth century the Boston public school was attempting to be all things to all children, dispensing moral and religious instruction along with book learning, the aim being to prepare students for the responsibilities of adulthood.

For Boston the decade of the 1840s was to be a period of rapid social change. The shift in population from farm to factory, the enormous influx of immigrants, the concentration of wealth in the hands of the few, with poverty the lot of the many, caused Horace Mann and other educational reformers to view the social role of the public school as one of maintaining social stability. In Mann's mind, this state of flux made public education imperative, and he drove himself relentlessly in the cause, travelling the length and breadth of the state time after time, speaking almost daily, gathering ideas and data for the *Common School Journal*.

Mann, however, was ever a practical reformer, impatient with theoretical discussions, thus when Elizabeth Peabody tried to urge certain of Emerson's philosophies upon him he replied with irritation, "Oh these Reformers and Spiritualizers who do everything well on paper! They can tell exactly how a road ought to be laid between here and New Orleans, but can they lay it?" The common school mission, as he saw it, was to produce moral individuals, responsible adults, loyal citizens, productive workers; there was little time for philosophizing.

While Boston possessed the financial resources as well as the public support for building an excellent system of public schools, rural and village schools generally fared poorly by comparison. They suffered from lack of funds and from public apathy, resulting in inadequate schools and incompetent teachers. Small wood-frame, one room schoolhouses often accommodated as many as a hundred children, crowded onto wooden benches, disciplined by harsh instructors wielding birch rods, causing Mann to write "there is more suffering endured by our children in them, than by prisoners in our jails and prisons." As for poor teaching, he asked, "shall those who despair of success in any employment be allowed to take up school-keeping as an ultimate resource?"

Mann himself, having passed his early years in such a schoolhouse, regretted in later life the few and miserable books for children, the poor teachers, and the fact that "until the age of fifteen I had never been to school more than eight or ten weeks in a year." The poet Whittier, too, was to recall his own childhood in such a school, the memory perhaps softened by the passage of time:

> Still sits the school-house by the road,
> A ragged beggar sleeping;
> Around it still the sumacs grow,
> And blackberry vines are creeping.

One of Mann's goals at this time was to publish a series of standard literary texts for school libraries around the district. Upon hearing this, Elizabeth Peabody, ever ready to promote the interests of her family and friends, recommended Hawthorne's *Twice-Told Tales*. What Mann had in mind for his schoolchildren, however, was literature heavily laced with moral and practical lessons, "nearer home to duty and business." When he raised the same objections to Richard Henry Dana's recently published and immensely popular *Two Years Before the Mast*, suggesting to the author that he rewrite it to include more geographical and moral instruction, the thoroughly annoyed Dana wrote that Mann was "a school master gone crazy."

Meanwhile, Mann was becoming more and more in demand as a lyceum speaker. In early 1840 he traveled to New York to give a series of lectures for the New York Mercantile Library Association. He was in distinguished company, for Longfellow and Emerson were scheduled for the series as well. Longfellow at that time was in a despondent mood, weary of the demands of the classroom and disappointed in love, so that the New York sojourn was a welcome respite. He found the cosmopolitan atmosphere there much to his liking, a pleasant contrast to the provincialism of Boston and Cambridge. After his return home he sank deeper into his personal slough of despond, writing to a friend in New York to ask about his prospects for earning a living there. His friend replied:

> To a poet it is useless to talk of positive happiness. Think of Halleck toiling at Mr. Astor's books - carrying forward million after million to page after page, and this another's wealth. Think of him living in this bustling city where God is worshipped and genius neglected -always poor among the stupid rich. He one of the victors in the great Tournament of this age, toiling up and down Broadway until his hair turns grey amidst the blind and shallow crowds that know him not! Then reflect upon the peaceful spot in which you are fulfilling your destiny - surrounded by poor scholars whose riches resemble your own - leading a life of toil not unenlivened by Romance.

Longfellow took his friend's advice, continuing to write

the poems that, whatever their subjects, so captured his young country's state of mind at that moment in her history. He was a born poet, writing of things his countrymen knew and felt and they rewarded him with literary success unknown before in America. He was even to know the hopeless "positive happiness" of which his friend had written, for in 1843 he would marry Fanny Appleton.

One of the few discordant notes in the chorus of praise following publication of *Voices of the Night* was sounded by a young Philadelphia literary critic named Edgar Allan Poe. Poe had achieved some favorable notice for the macabre short stories he was writing, but it was as critic that he was to become best known during his lifetime. He objected to the elementary moralizing of Longfellow's poems; to him this was the "wrong" aim of poetry. Writing in *Graham's Magazine*, he compared what he considered Longfellow's second-hand moral convictions to those of Emerson, whose were so much more powerful for having been born of solitary and independent thinking. Poe's attacks on Longfellow were to become increasingly malicious over the years, reflecting, in part, his disdain of the Boston literary establishment which had ostracized him, while he sank deeper and deeper into dissipation and mental instability, dying in 1849 at the age of forty.

Meanwhile, like everyone else in Boston with literary interests, Father had come to know and enjoy the camaraderie to be found at James Fields' Old Corner Bookstore. Standing two and a half stories at Washington and School Streets, its rose-colored brick exterior, steep gambrel roof and small windowpanes of leaded glass lent it a charming yet fashionable London look. The main entrance on Washington Street opened into a large salesroom, some forty feet square. Beyond this was a narrow passageway, on either side of which were located the offices of the publishing firm of Ticknor & Fields.

The senior partner William D. Ticknor sat at his desk behind a wooden railing on the right-hand side directing the business affairs of the firm, while to the left, in a small space separated from the salesroom by a green curtain, James Fields held daily court. A witty, genial extrovert, Fields was nonetheless serious in his determination to create a great publishing house devoted to fine literature. Over the next two decades he would indeed become the premier American publisher-patron of American and English literature, entertaining the great and near great in his small office cluttered with papers and manuscripts, the walls covered with pictures and mementos. A friend wrote, "... he drew, as a magnet draws its own, every kind of man, poet and philosopher and historian and divine ..."

In the early years, however, the Old Corner Bookstore was little more than the entertaining hub of Boston's literary establishment. On any day one might find Longfellow or Hawthorne or Allston browsing through the latest Tennyson or Dickens or DeQuincey among the well-stocked English importations; or there was a section devoted to medical books, reflecting an early interest of Ticknor's; or one might join Fields and one or two others for a lively luncheon at Mrs. Haven's Coffee House around the corner on School Street, a favorite rendezvous of friends and staff of the Old Corner.

Thus the momentous decade of the forties was underway, with its myriad currents and crosscurrents keeping Boston astir. Everywhere one looked there was activity, progress, the belief that all things were possible, and all problems solvable. Ominous clouds of dissension and discord had not yet begun to intrude upon the nation's consciousness. Still so young, America was coming into her own as a nation to be reckoned with; her long day of dependence on other lands was drawing to a close.

There were those who believed in progress, the railroad builders, the manufacturers, the educators, the politicians. Then there were those, listening to the siren-call of the Concord philosopher, who were dissatisfied with the outward world and had turned to exploring the inner life of thought and sentiment. They read their Keats and Tennyson and wrote their poetry, relied on their intuitions and wished to "be", not to "do".

Old Corner Bookstore; E.P. Dutton; Ticknor and Fields; Boston 1866
Source: Ticknor and Fields

There was the nether-world Hawthorne, writing his shadowy, ghostly tales; there was the real-world Hawthorne, writing his *Universal History* and editing the *American Magazine*, before toiling away amid the steamy docks and coal dust of the Boston Custom House. He wished to marry his Sophia, and one did have to earn a living, as a practical matter. But none of these things concerned me as the summer of 1840 approached, for I was soon to be married.

## Chapter XIII

  I suppose every bride awakens on her wedding day certain of Heaven's blessing on such a felicitous union as hers, and I was no exception. Thunderclouds had rumbled and flashed across the sky overnight, driving rain hard against the windows, but now the sun shone brightly upon a world that looked freshly scrubbed for the occasion. How could I not think that such a glorious morning was a happy omen for George and me?
  Emilie said I looked as radiant as a bride should as she helped me into my simple white organza dress, tucked flowers into my hair, and waited nervously with me until Father came for me. The minister and the few guests were assembled in the front parlor when Father and I descended the stairs to stand before the fireplace banked with white dahlias and fern. My husband-to-be was looking at me with an expression of such tenderness that I feared for a moment for my composure, but Father put his hand over mine and all was well again as I turned to George to repeat my wedding vows.
  After the brief ceremony, champagne toasts, and Esther's resplendent wedding cake garnished with strawberries, George and I prepared to take our leave of the ones who meant most to us in the world. I embraced my beloved father, then dear Uncle Karl, who I sensed felt he was losing a daughter, too, then ever faithful Esther and Asa, now grown old, and lastly my sure and steady Emilie. With her luxuriant dark chestnut hair and expression of quiet strength I thought how much she

resembled our mother and somehow I found that very comforting. George helped me into the waiting carriage, and as it pulled away I looked back at the little group gathered in front of the house until they were out of sight. Then I turned to my husband, ready to begin a new life as Eliza Darby. Eliza Darby. How I loved the sound of it!

After a few idyllic days in the New Hampshire countryside, we returned to Boston, driving directly to Mrs. Clarke's boardinghouse at No. 3 Somerset Court, close by the State House, where George had taken rooms. Mrs. Clarke's was known for genteel accommodations; it was the house where Elizabeth and Mary Peabody were living and keeping school when they first met Horace Mann. He was still suffering then from grief over the death of his young wife, and came there to find, as had been recommended to him by a friend, a "cheerful home" and "pleasant companions".

Once settled in at Mrs. Clarke's, George set to work again on his novel, which was progressing well he thought, and I returned to West Street each afternoon to teach pupils or to practice, as the habit was so thoroughly ingrained that I felt at a loss if I did not spend three or four hours a day at the piano. The Harvard Musical Society had engaged me for a recital in the spring and I knew that I could not let my repertoire slide too far from performance level. Besides, Uncle Hugo had sent, along with one of his regular letters from Leipzig, a collection of delightful short piano pieces by Robert Schumann entitled *Kinderscenen*. I wished to introduce them at the April recital, but they needed more work before performing them for that discriminating audience.

For some time Uncle Hugo had been urging an ambitious project, a life of Goethe, upon Father, regularly sending biographical material he was gathering along with his letters. We always welcomed news from Leipzig, but November brought the unhappy report of the estrangement between Clara Wieck and her father over his bitter opposition to her marriage to Schumann. Herr Wieck felt he had not made Clara the greatest woman pianist in Europe to have her throw it away on domesticity with a man he considered an eccentric ne'er do-well, and had tried to block it with every means at his disposal. But the event had finally taken place in September on Clara's twenty-first birthday, when her father's consent was no longer necessary. Despite the strain of the circumstances, Uncle Hugo reported that the couple appeared blissfully happy, with Clara going on with her concertizing as before. I hoped that the sad affair would soon be resolved as I cherished only the fondest memories of them all.

During this same time, Father offered to copy the manuscript of George's novel as it progressed, having heard the story of Thomas Carlyle's lending the partially completed manuscript of his monumental work, *The French Revolution* to a London friend to read, only to have it thrown into the fireplace by his friend's servant, thinking it was scrap. To Carlyle's credit, it did not end his sanity or the friendship, and he began once again to write what was to be his greatest literary masterpiece, bringing him success and acclaim and an end to a long struggle with poverty. George accepted Father's offer gratefully, having heard the story, too.

Late in November George and I attended a concert by the newly founded Academy of Music orchestra. It ambitiously attempted the Beethoven First and Fifth Symphonies in its first season, but they were so poorly played that I came away with a headache, wondering if America would ever have an orchestra to compare with that of the Gewandhaus. How I longed for that glorious sound! But Father, ever philosophical, said, "It's a start." Meanwhile, I decided I would be content with the much more satisfying presentations of the Handel and Haydn Society.

Thus the first winter of my marriage passed. No matter what the temperature outside, I basked in the warmth of our happiness, while my husband prepared his lessons or worked on his novel, and I taught my pupils and memorized the *Kinderscenen*. Often we walked to West Street to have supper with Father and Emilie, a welcome respite from the chatter of our fellow boarders around the dining table at Mrs. Clarke's. Father kept busy reading the biographical material on Goethe that Uncle Hugo sent, while copying George's book as each chapter was finished. Emilie told us she planned to give up her schoolroom at the end of the year to teach in a public school, preferring one in the poorest section of Boston. I thought how fortunate her students would be, for I knew there would be pictures on the wall and a vase of flowers on her desk and no birch rod.

One sunny Sunday afternoon in early April George and I were strolling through the Common, enjoying the first hints of spring, stopping to look for some sign of emerging leaves on the majestic Old Elm. Not finding any, we walked on toward Beacon Street, the copper dome of the State House straight ahead presiding over the Common from the Beacon Street side. This stately building was the greatest contribution to Boston and to the state of Massachusetts by America's foremost architect during the first decades after the Revolution.

Charles Bulfinch had been born into one of Boston's wealthiest families in 1763, attended Boston Latin School and Harvard College, and in 1785 sailed for Europe to embark upon a two year grand tour. He admired the neoclassic styles of the new English architecture, and upon returning to Boston spent the next several years designing the Massachusetts and Connecticut state houses, churches, public monuments, a theatre, a hotel, and a number of private homes, while serving as head of the Board of Selectmen for many years. In 1817 he was appointed by President Monroe who admired the Massachusetts State House, as architect of the Capitol in Washington. The next several years Bulfinch spent there supervising the completion of the building, returning to Boston in 1829 where he was to live, honored and revered, until his death in 1844.

As we turned toward home George said to me, "Eliza, I have had a letter from my father asking if I can take care of some family business in Albany, as he has not been well and cannot attend to it himself. I would like to see him and take my manuscript for him to read, so I have asked for a short leave from Harvard beginning next week. I will visit Father in New York for a few days, then take a steamer up the Hudson to Albany, and expect to be home again within a fortnight." A fortnight! That sounded like an eternity for our first separation since our marriage.

"I plan to see James Fields about publishing my book as soon as I get back, since I am only two or three chapters from completion. If it should prove even moderately successful, I think we can leave boardinghouse living behind us and move to a house of our own." Just then we were under the great spreading branches of the Old Elm again and I stopped, took his hand, and said, "We are going to need a house of our own before long, one that will have room for a nursery." He stood there looking at me with those intense dark eyes, then began slowly, "Eliza, you mean..." "Yes," I replied softly, "we are expecting a child." He picked me up and whirled me around, to the amusement of other strollers near-by, laughing, "Now my book has to be a success!"

On the morning of his departure we stood alone in Mrs. Clarke's small parlor to say our goodbyes. "A fortnight is a very short time, Eliza, then I will be home and you can announce our good news to the rest of mankind if you wish." Then growing serious he said, "You must take very good care of yourself while I'm gone. Do you think you should go through with the recital? Will it be too strenuous for you?" Smiling at his anxious expression, I replied, "Of course I will go through with the recital; in fact, I'm glad to have it to do while you're away. I will concentrate my thoughts on that so I won't miss you so much." At the door he took my hands, drew me to him, and whispered, "I love you more than anything in life, Eliza." As I watched him walk away I thought I must surely be the most blessed woman alive, to have such a man love me and to be carrying his child. Then I walked up the stairs to our silent, empty rooms.

That night I lay in my bed thinking about names for our baby to submit for George's approval when he returned. I

The Massachusetts State House,
designed by Charles Bulfinch,
in a stereograph image, circa 1862,
before the addition of wings.
Source: United States Library of Congress

decided on George Frederick, for its father and mine, if it should be a boy; if a girl, I liked Emilie Elizabeth, George's mother's name having been Elizabeth. Feeling very satisfied with my choices, I fell soundly asleep. The next morning I arose early and walked briskly across the Common in the crisp mid-April air, anticipating with pleasure Esther's incomparable cinnamon buns.

At breakfast Father told Emilie and me that Asa had come to him to say that he and Esther felt it was time for them to return to New York, wishing to live out the rest of their days among their family members there. Emilie and I, of course, could scarcely imagine our household without them, their having been a part of our lives from the time we first moved into the big house on Broadway so many years ago. That somehow set me thinking, as we talked, about beginnings and endings; how often in life it seemed that as one circumstance ends another begins, though in the present example, the others were not aware of it yet. Then I decided it was too early in the morning for philosophizing and got up from the table to go practice.

My recital for the Harvard Musical society went better than I had dared hope. Henry Longfellow was in the audience, as was Waldo Emerson. Elizabeth Peabody came with Margaret Fuller and their friend Sarah Clarke, our fellow inmate at her mother's boardinghouse and an accomplished artist; she was studying painting with Washington Allston, whose white head I noticed near the front row. There were other familiar faces, many of whom greeted me afterwards, expressing their particular enjoyment of Schumann's *Kinderscenen*, having never heard it played before.

The next afternoon I was seated at the piano in the West Street parlor just finishing a lesson, when I became aware that Father was standing in the doorway. The expression on his face alarmed me and I remained seated, afraid to stand, while my young pupil said goodbye to me and hurried out of the room past him. A feeling of unspeakable dread came over me as he walked slowly toward me. "Eliza ... Eliza, there has been an accident ... a terrible accident." He stood looking down at me now with his hand on my shoulder, and there was such pain in his eyes that I began to tremble and looked away. "The boiler of the steamer exploded and the boat broke up and sank too quickly for ... Eliza, there were no survivors." I sat too stunned to speak for a few moments, then slowly the words came, "No, Father, that is not possible ... that cannot possibly be true ... you are mistaken ... I am going to have a child ..." Now Emilie had entered the room and stood beside him, struggling for composure, and Father repeated gently, "Eliza, there were no survivors."

A wave of nausea swept over me and I thought I would faint, but somehow I managed to ask if they would leave me alone for a little while and, after hesitating, they both turned and left the room. My trembling hands went to the keyboard as if by their own power and the first plaintive notes of the slow movement of the Chopin E minor Concerto began to fill the parlor. I don't know how long I sat there, playing-on and on, unable to stop, starting again each time I had played it through until, finally, the room began to turn round and round and I fell from the bench into a crumpled heap on the floor, only vaguely aware that Father and Emilie were bending over me.

Now it was I who sat still and silent in my room, unable to comprehend my incomprehensible loss, unable, even, to cry out in anguish. I wanted to run screaming, to beat my fists against something, anything, but instead I sat silently while others attended me as we once had attended Father. But through the churning depths of my mind I knew that I must have George's baby; that alone would give me reason to go on with life without him, and slowly strength and awareness began to return.

## Chapter XIV

George Frederick Darby was born on an autumn day in 1841 just as the leaves were reaching their peak of blazing glory. As I held him in my arms for the first time the room glowed red in the late afternoon sun, reflecting deep crimson leaves of an old maple tree outside my window. This was my favorite time of the year. I could look out beyond the garden walls and marvel at nature's palette displayed amidst the neighboring rooftops - all red, russet and gold against the gentler October sky - while I marveled at the tiny bundle sleeping at my breast.

Esther and Asa had stayed on until the baby was born and we could find someone to replace them - as if they could be replaced. Father had not kept the carriage and horses in Boston, so we would require only a cook and housekeeper now. Meanwhile Esther sat by the hour rocking and singing to the baby, while Father came into the room several times a day just to stand and look at him, making me feel sometimes quite like a bystander in the whole affair. But once I began to be up and about, they reluctantly relinquished possession more and more to his mother.

I was back in my room on West Street - to stay, I supposed. Father and Emilie had moved my belongings from Mrs. Clarke's, so it looked as if I had never left. I had shut the memory of the accident that took my husband from me so completely from my mind that I imagined he had only gone away and would be returning in due time. Thus October passed, and before the first snow of November fell it was time to say goodbye to Asa and Esther. Father had hired a pleasant Scotswoman named Mary to look after the house, the baby and me, and I found myself wondering if she knew any lovely old Highland songs with the words set to them by Robert Burns. But even if she had, our household would never be quite the same without the two who had been a part of it for as long as I could remember. Promising to send regular reports of the baby's progress, Father, Emilie, and I stood on the brick sidewalk watching them drive away, their worldly possessions piled into the cart behind them, until the two gray heads could be seen no more.

For some weeks now Father had been hard at work on his life of Goethe, or so I thought as I looked in on him from time to time, writing at the desk in his study. Having been married to a writer, I knew better than to disturb him while he was working, so I merely paused in the doorway, then went on my way. Finally, one evening he called me in and when he looked up I was startled at his expression. Were those tears in his eyes? "Eliza, I have just finished George's book." Feeling my knees weaken, I sat down in his great leather chair as he continued, "I took the copy I had made of his manuscript to Ticknor and Fields some time ago and they think it is a fine piece of work. I told them I thought I could finish the last two chapters, as George had discussed with me how he intended it to end. I hope I have done it justice."

I went to him and put my arms around his neck, too overcome with emotion to say anything more than a barely audible "Thank you, Father." Looking down again, he said quietly, "It is very small repayment for the debt I owe him, Eliza. He gave me back my life." I ran upstairs to my room, took my baby from his crib, and with my lips close to his warm soft cheek, I whispered to him that his father's book was soon to be published and how proud and happy we would be, for I was sure it would be a great success. "And someday you will take up where he left off and write wonderful books, too. I know it, I *know* it."

A first edition of 1,000 copies was published in January and sold so quickly that a second printing was issued in February, a third in March. The reviews were almost without exception favorable, even Poe's, and overnight, it seemed, George Darby had become a famous author. How could he know? How could I tell him? Though it was I alone who silently basked in his success, I never for a moment forgot that it was *his* success, nor did Father, who would take no credit whatsoever for the beautifully written ending. By summer James Fields told me that the book was doing well in England, too, but the absence of international copyright laws meant that I would realize no financial benefit from its European sales. Pirating books was common practice by publishers on both sides of the ocean then; nevertheless, the book's success in America assured me of financial security enough. I would not be dependent upon Father for my son's education and for that I was very grateful.

In July, Hawthorne and Sophia Peabody were married in the parlor of 13 West Street, leaving directly after the ceremony for Concord to begin married life in the venerable gray parsonage there known as the Old Manse. This was the house in which Emerson's ancestor, the Reverend William Emerson, had witnessed from a window in his upstairs study the first shots fired in the Revolution. The three years spent in the old Manse were to be the happiest of Hawthorne's life. There, in the silent, tranquil atmosphere of rivers, woods, and fields - silent, that is, until the railroad arrived with its rumbling, whistling presence - Hawthorne fished, grew vegetables, and delighted in the miracles that artistic Sophia wrought in the old house with her paintbrush. And he wrote. These stories were written on a larger scale than his earlier tales and sketches, but still somber despite his outward happiness; such stories as *the Hall of Fantasy or Earth's Holocaust,* satirizing the gods his countrymen had set up to worship. Yet Hawthorne was no less skeptical of the reformers than he was of the values of the outside world; the human heart - therein lay the source of the world's misery. Reform from within - that was the only kind he understood.

The following May the Peabody parlor was once again the scene of a wedding, this time that of Mary Peabody and Horace Mann. Mann had been given leave of absence from his duties as Secretary of the Board of Education to study educational systems abroad, and in his practical way, had asked Mary to accompany him as his wife, thus combining his educational mission with a honeymoon. Of all the school systems he visited he was most impressed by those of Germany and Scotland. After several months he returned, determined to fuse the best of what he had learned in Europe with his native republican system, though he returned, also, with new and grave doubts about the future direction of his country. Was it wise to place political power in the hands of all the people? The Europeans' answer was a resounding NO. A friend expressed their concerns in a letter:

> The enlightened Germans who know your country have again and again made this remark to me. "You," said they, "teach that national happiness can be reached only thro' national education, intelligence, and morality. The United States are trying to experiment whether this condition can be reached by placing power in the hands of the ignorant masses. In Germany, especially in Prussia, we are trying to experiment whether we cannot reach it sooner and with less intermediate evil by placing power in the hands of the moral and enlightened, and employing it for the enlightenment and civilization of the masses with a view to giving them political power in proportion to their attainments in knowledge and morality! "Time, they say, will show which plan will succeed best, but in the interim, so far as America has gone, we prefer the steady peaceful morality of our own system, to the turmoil, dishonesty and mobbish tyranny of the Americans."

Sophia Peabody Hawthorne
Etching by Stephen Alonzo Schoff
Source: Boston Museum of Fine Arts

Mann felt a new urgency in his mission; he was convinced that the future of republicanism was bound to public education, thus the future rested on him and those who shared his belief that with a system of public education similar to those of the best of Europe, the triumph of republicanism was still possible. The alternative was political anarchy. He wrote to a friend, "If I had a few thousand dollars I could, very perceptively hasten the millennium. God having time enough on His own hands lets these things drag along strangely; but I confess I am so constituted that I feel in a hurry."

Not many weeks after the marriage of Mary Peabody and Horace Mann another wedding of note took place in the parlor of the Appleton mansion at 39 Beacon Street. After seven long years of disappointment and frustration, Henry Longfellow was married to Fanny Appleton. And, as if in reward for his patient forbearance, little was to disturb the serenity of his happiness until her tragic death almost eighteen years later. Cultivated, sensitive and intelligent, she was the ideal wife in this ideal partnership. Oliver Wendell Holmes once remarked in passing Craigie House that, "those who lived there had their happiness so perfect that no change ... could fail to be for the worse ..." Hawthorne, too, wrote, "Longfellow appears ... to be no more conscious of any earthly or spiritual trouble than a sunflower is of which lovely blossom he, I know not why, reminded me."

During these years Longfellow did not share Mann's fretful anxiety about his country's future, writing to a European friend:

> The idea, the meaning of America is very grand. She is working out one of the highest problems in the "celestial mechanics" of man. We must not be too impatient nor chide too harshly if in doing this she sometimes assumes an ungainly attitude; or have our teeth set on edge because the slate-pencil scratches a little.

Longfellow was steeped as few Americans were in European

culture, yet no other poet touched such a responsive American chord as he did; no one else was to achieve a more harmonious blending of the Old World with the New:

> A youth was there, of quiet ways,
> A student of old books and days,
> To whom all tongues and lands were known,
> And yet a lover of his own.

Father and I were pleased to accept an invitation to supper at Craigie House on an evening following one of Fanny Kemble's Shakespeare readings. Father would have been invited because of his acquaintance with the host; I was not sure whether I was included because of my own small reputation as a concert pianist or because I had now acquired a measure of vicarious celebrity as the widow of George Darby. But for whatever reason, I thoroughly enjoyed the evening of gracious hospitality in that beautiful house, surrounded by *objets d'art* and books, thousands of books. After supper Longfellow presented Mrs. Kemble a sonnet he had composed for the occasion, the last lines of which read:

> O happy poet! by no critic vexed!
> How must thy listening spirit now rejoice
> To be interpreted by such a voice!

## Chapter XV

By the mid-forties I had begun to feel that Father's trust in America's cultural future might at last be justified. Perhaps he was no longer one of only a few who seemed to recognize "the value of culture in making a society whole." Certainly it seemed so in Boston, and I suppose one could say that the three adult members of the Rupp family of West Street were in the thick of it, each of us adding our own individual ingredients to the cultural pot that seemed so near the boiling point.

Margaret Fuller's "conversations" at Elizabeth Peabody's bookshop had ended, and after a summer spent travelling in the West, she had gone to New York to write for Horace Greeley's *Tribune* about Germans and Swedes flocking to the prairies and Indians clustered around the lakes and streams of Illinois, Ohio and Wisconsin. Now the literary critic for the *Tribune*, she interpreted the more important American and European writers of the day, interlaced with her opinions on a wide variety of subjects. She wrote, for example, "The superficial diffusion of knowledge, unless attended by a corresponding deepening of its sources, is likely to vulgarize rather than raise the thought of a nation, depriving it of another sort of education through sentiments of reverence, and leading the multitude to believe themselves capable of judging what they but dimly discern." Margaret Fuller had left Emerson's cloud-land for Earth.

The 13 West Street bookshop itself had closed, Miss Peabody packing her books, pamphlets, and old issues of the *Dial* for storing at the back of the apothecary shop. Her business, never more than barely able to meet expenses, had declined, owing no doubt to the ascent of the Old Corner Bookstore under James Fields' stewardship as the congenial hub of literary Boston. Too, both her sisters were married and gone and her mother was now too frail to help any longer in tending the shop. Then there were the other shops beginning to encroach upon West Street, making it a less desirable location than it had been before.

Washington Allston had died and I missed his gentle presence at my recitals for the Harvard Musical Society. Father had attended the funeral in Cambridgeport, joining the procession of mourners that walked to Cambridge at twilight to stand with bowed heads as the coffin was lowered into the grave. Standing there in the darkness, illuminated only by students bearing torches, they must all have felt grateful, as Father did, for the legacy of art, letters and generous friendship left by this uncommon man. The American sculptor Horatio Greenough who, like Story, was to spend most of his life in Italy, wrote of him, "He taught me first how to discriminate - how to think, how to feel. Before I knew him I felt strongly but blindly, as it were; and if I should never pass mediocrity, I should attribute it to my absence from him ..."

Greenough himself had been born in Boston, setting out for Rome upon his graduation from Harvard in 1825. In 1832 Congress awarded him the first grand commission given to any sculptor for a monumental sculpture of George Washington to be placed in the Rotunda of the Capitol. Eight years in the creation, it reached Washington in 1841. It brought Greenough both fame and ridicule, for his version of the father of his country was seated on a throne wearing a Roman toga, bare-chested, his outstretched left hand holding a Roman sword in a scabbard. One amused, or not so amused, observer remarked that Washington was proclaiming, "Here is my sword - my clothes are in the Patent Office yonder."

Greenough, distressed more by the effect of the harsh

lighting of the Rotunda on his huge statue than by the ridicule, petitioned Congress to remove it to the Capitol lawn, where it sits now, half-naked, in rather forlorn indignity while puddles of rain collect in its deeply cut drapery. Despite the criticism, Congress would award Greenough another commission in 1847, this time for a group of figures of a pioneer family and an Indian, entitled "The Rescue." Although not installed at the east side of the capitol until after his death in 1851, by then his sculptures and his collection of essays on art, architecture and aesthetics had earned him the title of founding father of America's first school of sculpture.

These years of the middle and late forties were to witness a great outpouring of literature from Boston and its environs. In 1845 Longfellow produced an immense anthology entitled *The Poets and Poetry of Europe*, the first large-scale introduction of foreign literature to the United States. Hawthorne brought out a new edition of *Twice Told Tales* which included twenty-one more short stories than in the earlier edition. It was a critical, though not a financial success, Poe writing in *Graham's Magazine*, "Mr. Hawthorne's distinctive trait is invention, creation, imagination, originality - a trait which, in the literature of fiction, is positively worth all the rest ..." Hawthorne, now with a wife and baby to support and in need of a steady income, obtained through the efforts of his friends an appointment as Surveyor of the port of Salem, and in 1846 he and Sophia bade farewell to the Old Manse.

In the same year another collection of his stories, a two-volume edition of *Mosses from an Old Manse* was published, again bringing him critical acclaim but very little financial reward. One critic lamented, "It is a waste of a kind of genius, which we cannot well spare, to shut Nathaniel Hawthorne in a custom house." Poe's review this time faulted Hawthorne's penchant for allegory, but attributed his lack of recognition by the public and the critics to his being a "poor man" who could not buy literary favors; nor was he, in Poe's view, a "ubiquitous quack" of the sort which seemed to him to thrive in American

The Rescue
By Horatio Greenough
Outside of the U. S. Capitol

culture.

Meanwhile in Concord, Henry Thoreau was finding it impossible to support himself by writing, due in large part to the limited appeal his nature writings had at that time. He had contributed a number of poems and essays to the *Dial* before its demise, but now he was at work on his first book, the fruit of his two year experiment in independent living in a hermit's cabin near Walden Pond. The book, entitled *A Week on the Concord and Merrimack Rivers*, was published after he left his hut in the woods, but was a resounding failure, dealing a severe blow to his literary ambitions. He returned to odd jobs such as ditching and surveying to support himself, while continuing to keep a journal in which were recorded his thoughts and observations for use as material for his essays and books. Almost a decade was to pass before he would finally achieve success with the book that was to prove his masterpiece, *Walden*.

In 1846 Longfellow joined the ranks of authors published by Ticknor & Fields, solidly establishing the firm's reputation as one of the leading publishers of the English-speaking world. The following November Longfellow's book-length poem *Evangeline* was published. Its success was immediate and sensational, running to six printings by January. No other poem ever published enjoyed such popular acclaim - or such sales. Hawthorne had given Longfellow the idea for the poem and, producing little of his own work at this period, wrote a review of it for the *Salem Advertiser*. Longfellow responded, "I thank you for resigning to me that '*Legend of Acady*'! This success I owe entirely to you, for being willing to forego the pleasure of writing a prose tale, which many people would have taken for poetry, that I might write a poem that many people take for prose."

In the last years of these momentous forties Horace Mann was finally to see positive progress from his years of battle for public education, later writing, "The Common School cause in Massachusetts was so consolidated - as the French say about their republicanism - that I felt nothing could overturn it. It was only annoyances and obstructions that we had to look after." But he was battle-weary and ready to step aside. He wrote, "Tired, jaded, exhausted, devitalized, extinct, the first news on my arrival here, is that I am advertised to Lecture, tomorrow evening ... But it cannot be helped, and I must steam up the old machinery once more, and make it go." Then Fate stepped into Mann's life when John Quincy Adams, now eighty-one, collapsed on the floor of the U.S. House of Representatives in February 1848, dying the next day. In April Mann was elected to the vacant seat by a landslide and after a twelve-year absence, he returned to politics.

For me, personally, the most memorable event of that memorable decade's waning years was the founding of the Germania Orchestra. The German uprisings of 1848, part of the general unrest throughout continental Europe at the time, caused music to languish there to such a degree that poverty forced many excellent musicians to leave, a number of them immigrating to the United States. The orchestra traveled about the country, playing works of the greatest German composers from Haydn to Mendelssohn, its fifty or so members and leaders all artists of the first rank; their concentration on Germanic works was to greatly influence American attitudes toward "standard repertory" of orchestral music.

Fortunately for Boston, most of their concerts were played there, and I rejoiced that at last, at long last, here was an orchestra that brought back memories of the Gewandhaus. Over the next few years I would perform periodically with that admirable ensemble, playing a half dozen or so different concertos, but there was one I would never play in public. The slow movement of the Chopin E minor Concerto was my own. How could I possibly share with others music so personal, music that I had turned to in my darkest hours? Chopin's F minor Concerto I would, and did, play; the E minor, never.

During these years, Emilie's wish to teach in a poor section of Boston had been realized. The Boylston School had been built in 1819 in a section of the city called Fort Hill, a shady tree-lined park area overlooking the harbor. The homes of some of Boston's leading families were located there then, and the school was the realization of the ideal of a city school in a rural school setting with its spacious grassy playground, unlike the badly located, poorly ventilated, multi-use structures that housed most of Boston's public schools.

By the early forties, however, the enormous influx of Irish immigrants into Boston had changed the character of Fort Hill. The wealthier citizens had moved away, and into the once shady park were now crowded businesses, warehouses, and the shanties of the poor. Speculators began carving out portions of the hill and filling them with wooden tenements, often housing several families in what one investigator described as "a perfect hive of human beings, without comforts and mostly without common necessaries." It was into this environment that Emilie once again ventured, this time without the protection of Asa, to teach the children of poor and ignorant Irishmen.

By the mid-forties there were nineteen public grammar schools in Boston, five for boys only, five for girls only, eight mixed - into which category Boylston fell - and one for Negro children. They were generally two-story square buildings with one large schoolroom on each floor, holding 200 or more children sitting in long rows on wooden benches. School sessions were year round, broken by periodic holidays, with a schoolmaster in control of each school. Students were divided into four recitation groups, separating the younger from the older ones, with each teacher responsible for some sixty students. The masters usually taught only the upper classes, the teachers the lower; the masters were paid $125 monthly, male teachers $32 and female teachers $20. I wondered if Emilie could adjust to such circumstances after her light and cheerful West Street schoolroom and her fifteen young ladies from genteel families. But if anyone could perform miracles under such conditions, I knew it would be Emilie.

And perform miracles she did over the years. With meagre equipment, large classes, the constant shifting from place to place of many of the impoverished immigrants of Fort Hill, the truancy, the neglect; with all that she managed to teach most of her children something, some a great deal, from the broad range of curriculum. Before the boys left school at fourteen, the girls at sixteen, they had been exposed to spelling, reading, grammar, geography, arithmetic and handwriting. Some of the schools taught, in addition, history, natural philosophy, algebra, geometry and bookkeeping.

Emilie never forgot the impassioned words of Horace Mann on that Fourth of July morning; nor those of another educator, George B. Emerson: "Unless they become inmates of our schools, many of them will become inmates of our prisons;" nor those of a young lawyer, Christopher Andrews, who said, "while we furnish subsistence to those whom intemperance and idleness have brought to destitution - while we erect asylums where reason may be restored to the shattered mind - while we enlarge prisons in which to punish the violators of the law - we should remember that some endeavors should be made to prevent others from requiring the same charities, and incurring the same penalties. Instead of standing merely by the fatal shoal to rescue the sinking crew, we should raise a warning signal to avert further shipwrecks." The means was public education.

## Chapter XVI

Looking back, 1850 stands out in relief as a watershed year. Never before had so many events and currents seemed to converge, so many hopes and fears commingled, so much optimism been leavened by a vague sense of foreboding about America's future. Horace Mann expressed it in writing to Mary from Washington, "There are dark clouds overhanging the future, and worse, they are full of lightning." American politics were turning increasingly bitter and rancorous.

But for me, I was content with my music and, most of all, with watching my son growing up. Now almost nine and a student at the Boston Latin School, he and his grandfather together were a joy to behold. From the time George was a baby Father had taken over the paternal role with ease and grace. So many times I had looked into his study to see him reading an oft-requested favorite bedtime story to George, settled snugly into his grandfather's lap in the great leather chair before the fireplace. So many times I had watched them walk away, a small chubby hand holding onto Father's, off on a sojourn to the Common, the child with dark eyes and tousled hair, the still handsome tall, erect man with the blue-gray eyes that seemed to see everything around him at once.

They were always talking together about important matters like the anthill under the great Old Elm in the Common or the different kinds of birds they spotted in its leafy branches. But what I loved most of all was to look into the study to see young George reading to his attentive grandfather the little stories and poems he had written in school. Occasionally there was a special poem for me which I carefully tucked away in a box of my most treasured possessions. He was so like his father that sometimes I felt frightened and wanted to put my arms around him to keep him from harm's way, but that feeling always passed quickly as I sent him off to school or play, watching until he was out of sight.

The greatest cultural event of 1850 was the publication by Ticknor & Fields of Hawthorne's exquisite first novel, *The Scarlet Letter*. Hailed by the literary world as the finest piece of imaginative writing yet produced in America, it was in every sense American, and it was welcomed as a novel belonging to the very forefront of great literature, equal to any that had been received from the other side of the ocean. After all the years of struggle, Hawthorne was at last a world-famous author.

James Fields had called on Hawthorne in Salem, hearing he was ill, and had departed with the manuscript of *The Scarlet Letter*, Hawthorne's calling after him as he was leaving, "It is either very good or very bad - I don't know which." The first edition of twenty-five hundred copies was an immediate success, followed in days by a second printing as large as the first, with subsequent editions stereotyped. Fields added *The Scarlet Letter* to his list of books with great pride, having already in that year the satisfaction of publishing two new volumes of Whittier, an American edition of Holmes' poems, all of Longfellow's poetry in a two-volume edition - so successful it was published year after year - and in two volumes the poetry of Robert Browning, first bringing him to the American public. Thus in 1850 Fields was the publisher of Tennyson, Browning, and DeQuincey from Europe; at home, of Hawthorne, Longfellow, Whittier, Holmes, and Lowell.

In 1850 the Hawthornes moved to Lenox in the tranquil Berkshires of Massachusetts, Hawthorne having been turned out of the Salem customhouse with a change of administrations in Washington. There, in a little red house by the side

Title Page, The Scarlet Letter
First Edition – Ticknor, Reed, and Fields, 1850

of the road he would receive a steady stream of visitors who stopped by to visit with the now-famous author, and he would write more during his two year residence there than at any period of his career. He began work on *The House of the Seven Gables* which Fields published in 1851 to even greater success than *The Scarlet Letter*, though the reviews proved to be more mixed. From this period came as well a third edition of *Twice Told Tales*, a new volume of previously uncollected stories in *The Snow Image*, and a collection of children's stories.

Soon after Hawthorne's arrival in Lenox, he became acquainted with Herman Melville who was living on a farm near Pittsfield and working on his novel *Moby Dick*. Melville had published several popular earlier books based on his youthful experiences as a roustabout sailor, but *Moby Dick* was to be his masterpiece, the fruit of his maturity. Published in 1851 it was, however, not well received and a subsequent novel, *Pierre*, was so savaged by the critics that his writing career was all but finished. His friendship with the reserved Hawthorne was destined to be more than a little one-sided; he wrote an effusive, extravagant review of Hawthorne in the *Literary World*, comparing him to Shakespeare, and Hawthorne's influence, particularly in Melville's use of allegory in dealing with good and evil, courage, cowardice, and pride in *Moby Dick*, is much in evidence. His book was dedicated to Hawthorne.

For some years now Boston had been a favored stop for touring European virtuosos. By 1850 the musical taste of American concert audiences had begun to mature, but for a few years prior to mid-century they welcomed European virtuosos with open arms, and open pocket books, tending to equate technical brilliance with artistry, virtuosity with talent. Three of the most famous, the Norwegian violinist Ole Bull, who came for the first time in 1843, the German pianist Leopold de Meyer in 1845, and Austrian pianist Henri Herz the next year, thrilled American mass audiences with their technical feats and shallow salon pieces, becoming very rich in the process.

But in 1850 came one who captivated everyone who heard

Photograph of Herman Melville
Circa 1860
Source: Unknown, Public Domain

her. Jenny Lind, the "Swedish Nightingale," the operatic soprano who was a virtuoso in the very best sense of the word, made her Boston concert debut in late September. She drew such huge crowds during her two-year American tour that tickets were sold at auction, reaching an astonishing record high of $625. Father, Emilie and I attended her Boston concert and were enchanted, as was everyone else, by the purity and naturalness of her art. Longfellow wrote of her, "She is very feminine and lovely. Her power is in her presence, which is magnetic. Clear, liquid, heavenly sounds."

In 1850 Longfellow brought out a new volume of poems under the title *The Seaside and the Fireside.* One among the collection, "The Building of the Ship," spoke so directly and so eloquently to America's mingled hopes and fears as the country moved into the second half of the century that it inspired not only the literate public, but Lincoln, too, until all hope for peace was gone. Not long after its publication Fanny Kemble created a sensation one evening when, after a reading of *As You Like It,* she stepped from behind her red-covered reading desk to the front of the platform, book in hand, and stunned her audience with a dramatic and unscheduled reading of "The Building of the Ship." No one moved and no sound but her voice could be heard as, trembling and weeping, she began the final verse:

> Thou, too, sail on, O Ship of State!
> Sail on, O UNION, strong and great!
> Humanity with all its fears,
> With all the hopes of future years,
> Is hanging breathless on thy fate!
> We know what Master laid thy keel,
> What Workmen wrought thy ribs of steel,
> Who made each mast, and sail, and rope
> What anvils rang, what hammers beat,
> In what a forge and what a heat
> Were shaped the anchors of thy hope!

Fear not each sudden sound and shock,
'Tis of the wave and not the rock;
'Tis but the flapping of the sail,
And not a rent made by the gale!
In spite of rock and tempest's roar,
In spite of false lights on the shore,
Sail on, nor fear to breast the sea!
Our hearts, our hopes are all with thee,
Our hearts, our hopes, our prayers, our tears,
Our faith triumphant o'er our fears,
Are all with thee, are all with thee!

The audience sat in silence for a moment, then as if one, rose to their feet for a prolonged ovation for the reader and the author, who once more had articulated so perfectly what the man in the street or on the farm or in the lecture hall thought and felt but could not express so well. What did it matter to them that as a poet he neither soared high nor plumbed deep - he was *their* poet.

# Chapter XVII

The opening of the magnificent Boston Music Hall in 1852 was a long-awaited event for the city and for me. Boston had long needed a new and larger hall, having outgrown the Odeon, and now, at last, it stood complete in all its grandeur. All the musical societies of the city participated in the brilliant opening night concert, together with two famous European singers who happened to be touring in the United States at the time. What an experience it was to sit amidst the huge crowd filling every one of the 2,700 seats, listening to some of the world's greatest music in the country's newest, largest and finest hall. The building was set back off Winter and Tremont streets to lessen street noise; once inside, the effect of the lighting by jets of gas running around the cornice on all four sides was breathtaking.

I thought as I looked around how thrilling it would be to perform in such surroundings, and my opportunity was not long in coming. In early 1853 the Germania Orchestra and the Handel and Haydn Society gave Boston its first hearing of the Beethoven Ninth, or great Choral, Symphony with resounding success. The program opened with the second piano concerto of Mendelssohn, for which I was soloist, but I fear my performance was soon forgotten in the wonder of the mighty Beethoven Ninth with its glorious choral ending.

I had heard the symphony once before in the Gewandhaus in Leipzig, and as I listened I vividly remembered the story Uncle

Interior View of the New Music Hall in Boston, 1852
Source: United States Library of Congress

Hugo had told me of the premier performance in Vienna in 1824, with Beethoven himself, now totally deaf, assisting. He had stood at the right of the conductor, intently watching the score throughout. At the end the audience broke into a thundering ovation, standing, stomping their feet, waving handkerchiefs. Not until the conductor took him by the sleeve and gently turned him to face the audience did Beethoven realize what a tumultuous reception he and his symphony were receiving. The ovation roared on and on as the greatest living composer of the time bowed again and again and again, hearing nothing. Remembering the story brought tears to my eyes as I listened in that splendid hall in Boston, just as it had all those years ago in the Clothier's Hall of Leipzig.

Another event of 1852 burst upon Boston and the entire nation like a skyrocket. *Uncle Tom's Cabin*, a book by Harriet Beecher Stowe, the wife of an obscure Bowdoin College professor, addressed the great and growing moral-political dilemma of the time, Negro emancipation. It had a runaway sale of 10,000 copies in the first week, reaching an astonishing quarter of a million books sold within nine months. Overwhelmed, Longfellow wrote, "How she is shaking the world with her *Uncle Tom's Cabin!*" The ground swell of moral indignation the book aroused was without any doubt a factor in the ever-increasing polarization of the country over the emancipation question. Before the book's popularity waned it had been translated into some twenty-three languages. Thereafter Mrs. Stowe lived the life of a woman of letters, writing other novels, none of which was to have the impact of her first.

In 1853 Hawthorne was appointed by his old friend and Bowdoin classmate, now President of the United States, Franklin Pierce, to the lucrative consulship at Liverpool. Pierce had asked Hawthorne to write his campaign biography during the election of 1852, and though Pierce's name was anathema to northern intellectuals, Hawthorne out of friendship did so. Pierce rewarded his loyalty with the consulship. In July Hawthorne and his family sailed for Europe, not to return until

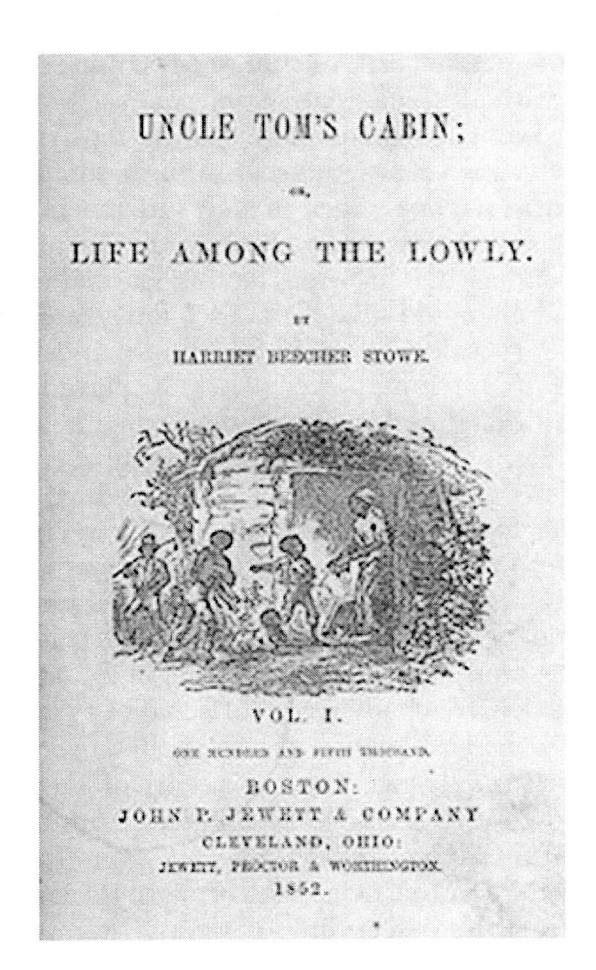

Title Page of Uncle Tom's Cabin
Illustrated by Hammatt Billings
First Edition, 1852

1860 to what he called the "miserable confusion" of American politics. During the years abroad he would travel extensively and write his last complete novel, *The Marble Faun*, before returning home to Concord, unsure of his country's future, in declining health and imaginative powers.

Another event of note in 1853 was the return of the first American virtuoso pianist and composer to achieve fame and celebrity in Europe. Born in New Orleans in 1829, Louis Moreau Gottschalk was sent to Paris at the age of thirteen to complete his musical education, having learned all that New Orleans teachers could give him. In a few years he was the rage of the Paris salons, praised by Chopin and Berlioz, piling triumph upon triumph everywhere he played. *La France Musicale* had exclaimed in amazement when he began playing his own piano pieces, "An American composer, *bon Dieu*!"

The reviews of his first concert after arriving in New York were ecstatic. Not so in Boston. John Sullivan Dwight in his *Journal of Music*, the most important musical magazine in America, praised his technique but criticized his repertoire, including his own pieces, as superficial: "what is the execution without some thought and meaning in the combinations to be executed?" He challenged Gottschalk to play some real music, but by then the pianist was so spoiled by years of adulation and self-indulgence that the quality of his playing had begun its downward slide. How different from my memory of the youthful Clara Wieck!

In 1854 letters from Uncle Hugo brought the tragic news of Robert Schumann's descent into insanity. The composer had entered a private asylum near Bonn where he would remain until his death in 1856. After her husband's breakdown, it became necessary for Clara to resume her concert career full-time in order to support her seven children. She began touring again, with a heavy schedule of formidable programs, playing every concert dressed in black, the great classical pianist who was never to yield to "popular" demands. The Austrian critic Hanslick wrote that she gave "a clear expression to each work in its characteristic musical style ... She could be called the greatest living pianist, rather than merely the greatest female pianist, were the range of her physical strength not limited by her sex ... Everything is distinct, clear, sharp as a pencil sketch." Through the great tragedy of her life she was to summon up her fullest powers as a woman and as an artist.

Longfellow resigned his professorship at Harvard in 1854 to devote himself exclusively to writing, and in 1855 came another enormously successful long poem, *The Song of Hiawatha*. Just as Cooper earlier had found romance in America's scanty past, so did Longfellow in his retelling of the Indian legends he had read, reshaping them to suit himself, softening and humanizing them, until his poem seemed to have been written through a golden autumn haze. Once again Longfellow had instinctively gauged the country's pulse, this time in the growing nationalism of the United States, and by extension, the interest in her past. Of his three long narrative poems, *The Courtship of Miles Standish*, published in 1858 probably became his best known. Where Hawthorne's depictions of Puritan New England were shadowy and somber, Longfellow's in *Miles Standish* were light and pastoral. Which was more real? Perhaps they both were.

James Fields was a widower when he married again in 1854. Annie Fields was seventeen years his junior, but it was to be the happiest of marriages, with Annie the perfect hostess for the constant entertaining that kept their elegant house on Beacon Hill filled with guests. They moved into the new house at 37 Charles street in 1856, and from then on it was a veritable salon in a New World that knew little of such things, filled with books, paintings, replicas of Greek and Roman statuary, marble busts of literary and stage personages, and the memorabilia collected by Fields over his years of friendship with the famous and near-famous. The serene and gracious Annie devoted herself to her house and its guests and, sharing her husband's genuine regard for literary people, made it the most famous gathering place in America.

The most impressive room was the upstairs library which

ran the entire length of the house, windows overlooking Charles Street at the front and at the back a sweeping view of the Charles River and the hills beyond. The room was filled with their collections and with furnishings of ornate Italian style. A massive grand piano occupied one wall at the center. I played for an occasional musicale in this room when the other guests could have been from anywhere - Cambridge, Concord, other areas of New England, New York, Philadelphia, England. Most were writers or critics, but there were singers, actors, playwrights, lawyers and Congressmen as well. All these same people, and more, could still be found on any day at the Old Corner, dropping in to look over the new offerings, or to chat with each other or with Fields in his small cluttered office behind the green curtains. In the hearty world of James Fields it was harder to see the gathering dark clouds, full of lightning, of which Horace Mann had written. But as the decade of the fifties waned, every American was forced to look, like it or not.

A widespread business panic in 1857 added to the general anxiety, the sense that the times were sick and beyond the ability of men to cure them. The whole temper of society, of business, of politics, was growing more and more uneasy, the atmosphere becoming heavy and ominous like the approach of a terrible storm, when all anyone can do is wait for it to strike with all its force and fury. My son was now at Harvard, and when I looked at him, the image of his father with his dark eyes and serious expression, I trembled for him and all the other young men at the very threshold of their lives. How many of them were to be sacrificed to this madness? Was this the best the politicians could do?

One gallant attempt at normalcy during this increasingly abnormal time was made by the Handel and Haydn Society when a great three-day Festival of Music was announced for May 1857. Modeled after those in Europe, the conductor Carl Zerrahn engaged the best singers and musicians from around the country, swelling the orchestra to an unprecedented seventy-eight members. It opened on the afternoon of May 22 with the Grand March from Wagner's *Lohengrin* followed that same evening by a stupendous performance of Handel's *Messiah*.

I could not have described the excitement of that evening better than the reviewer who wrote, "The Festival has at length wrought conviction in men's minds, that it is something honest, as it is rare and good ... a sincere Festival of Art, a presentation of grand music on a grand scale. The Music Hall is crammed with listeners in every seat, and standing place, and doorway, from floor to upper gallery. There is the utmost eagerness to hear the Handel Hallelujahs from that mighty chorus, and it is mightier than ever; the stage is packed as closely as the auditorium." It was said that the chorus numbered almost seven hundred.

Even with the enthusiasm aroused by the great success of the Festival, the inspiration to build upon its triumph, the undeniable proof that we could achieve the highest and the best - even with all that, the times had to be reckoned with, and the times could not be sung into health. As political and business anxieties increased, interest in the fine arts and in fine literature languished proportionately. Even at the Old Corner business had begun to slacken so noticeably by the end of the decade that, even with the addition of Emerson, Thoreau, and Julia Ward Howe, author of "The Battle Hymn of the Republic," to Fields' roster, Longfellow could observe, "The 'Corner' looks gloomy enough. Ticknor looks grim and Fields is fierce. Business is at a standstill. So much for war and books."

In mid-October 1859 a band of fanatical abolitionists led by the demented John Brown seized the United States arsenal at Harper's Ferry, Virginia. Brown's quick trial and subsequent execution on December 2nd unleashed the headlong course of events which followed, polarizing the country beyond all hope of reconciliation. Most Americans, including the man on whom the awesome burden was to fall most heavily, abhorred the anarchy and lawlessness Brown represented, but there were those, like the Concord Transcendentalists, who looked upon him as a hero and a martyr. Emerson, Thoreau,

Bronson Alcott, and Elizabeth Peabody spoke at a memorial service in the Concord Town Hall.

Thus the turbulent decade ended. Was everything of beauty and worth, everything that Father, Emilie and I had devoted our lives to, to count for nothing after all? Were the years of striving by so many, believing there could be, should be, more to America than factories, steamships and locomotives only a cruel joke in the end? Was the great American experiment itself to collapse in bloody failure – and not from an enemy without, but from some failure inherent in our system? These were the thoughts that weighed heavily upon me as the new year approached. Never before had a year been greeted with so much apprehension by so many Americans as the year 1860.

Harper's Ferry Incident
U.S. Marines Attacking the Firehouse which John Brown
used as a fort during his raid on Harper's Ferry.
Source: Harper's Weekly and the
United States Library of Congress

## Chapter XVIII

In the early evening of 29th June 1860, a violent storm roared through Boston. In its aftermath lay the debris of broken and uprooted trees, awnings torn from the fronts of business establishments, pieces of glass from windows unable to withstand the fury of the wind. Fortunately our house escaped serious damage, but I had feared for the old maple tree outside my window as its branches creaked and groaned and beat against the roof.

The next morning a rumor that the Old Elm was down spread quickly through the city. Hundreds of citizens, including Father and me, went to see for themselves, and a pathetic sight it was. The once mighty limbs lay broken and scattered about the ground, while what remained stood mutilated and shorn of its beauty and majesty. Those who gathered there gazed in silent disbelief at first, almost reverentially, as if mourning the sudden, unexpected loss of a dear friend. Then slowly people began picking up bits and pieces of the limbs and leaving, as if carrying away priceless relics of some ancient monument. Who among them had not played beneath its sheltering branches as a child; had not strolled there with a young love; had not discussed important or unimportant matters of business, politics or the weather there? Like the others I had memories of my own as I searched for a piece to carry home and treasure.

Young George Darby, meanwhile, graduated from Harvard. He had been named Class Poet, and at his commencement

Father, Emilie and I sat proudly listening while he expressed in inspired verse the hopes and aspirations of his generation in these fearful times. How could he speak so confidently, so optimistically of the future when he and his generation would be the ones called upon if it came to war? How could they think of the now almost certain conflagration looming ahead as a great and noble cause, to be resolved quickly, surely and triumphantly, with honor and glory? Couldn't they see that war was dirt and death and devastation, with both sides believing equally in their cause? I looked around at their young and earnest faces and I shuddered for them all.

After the ceremony we mingled with the other guests, visiting with friends, acquaintances and professors, accepting with thanks their praise of George's commencement poem. James Russell Lowell had succeeded Longfellow as Professor of modern languages and was himself a writer of considerable note. In addition, he edited the *Atlantic Monthly*, the most prestigious literary periodical of the moment. He mentioned that one of George's short stories would appear in the next issue, and I tried not to show my surprise, as in fact I knew nothing of it. As we walked home across the bridge I asked George why he had not told me news of such importance. "Professor Lowell was not aware that I wanted to surprise you, Mother. I had told Grandfather, but I wanted you to just open the magazine and find it there. Grandfather and I, of course, would be standing by to enjoy your reaction, with a bottle of champagne close at hand. But now that you know, why don't we stop off on the way home and celebrate my first published piece of writing - the first, I hope, of many!"

Abraham Lincoln of Illinois was elected President in November 1860. A few days later North Carolina seceded and in February 1861 a provisional government of the Confederate States of America was established. On the morning of April 12 Confederate forces opened fire on Fort Sumter in the Charleston harbor; Lincoln issued a call for 75,000 volunteers and the war to preserve the Union had begun. On the 17th a

Massachusetts regiment, the first in the nation to answer the call, began its march to the capital.

The great music of the Handel and Haydn Society was silenced. In its place were heard the drum and the fife in the streets, the bugle and trumpet, the cannons and the alarm-bells. But then an announcement came from the Society:

> The Handel and Haydn Society, desirous of contributing something toward the preservation of our common country, in this, its day of trial, will give a grand concert of miscellaneous patriotic and national music at the Boston Music Hall on Saturday evening, April 27. The entire proceeds will be handed over to the Governor of the Commonwealth for the purpose of arming and equipping troops in the service of the country.

The concert was a resounding success, with the patriotic songs brilliantly played and enthusiastically applauded. The great chorale sang some stirring Handel choruses, and then the audience joined in the noble strains of "America."

A few days later I was saying goodbye to a pupil at the door when I turned to see my son standing there in the blue uniform of the Union army. I could feel the color drain from my face as I realized the day I had dreaded so long had finally come. George came to me and put his arms around me, "Mother, the sooner we get this matter resolved the sooner we can all go on with our lives." "What about the books you are going to write?" I sobbed into his shoulder. "I will write them when I come back, better than they would have been. I promise you." I stood there watching him walk away and suddenly a great uncontrollable fear swept over me. Trembling and faint, I walked to the piano in the parlor, sat down on the bench and, just as on that terrible day twenty years before, my fingers began to move over the keys with the first plaintive notes of the Chopin E minor Concerto slow movement.

I had played no more than a few measures when I felt a

hand on my shoulder and I realized Father was standing beside me. "It is a beautiful day, Eliza. Why don't we go walk in the Common?" I got up slowly and we walked together up West Street without a word spoken, crossed Tremont and entered the gateway into the tender springtime green of the Common. There were children playing as usual, babies being pushed in carriages, men hurrying to and from their places of business. Presently we came to the battered remains of the once proud and mighty Old Elm.

We stood there looking at it in silence, each of us lost in our own thoughts, when suddenly Father called out, "Look, Eliza! On the westerly side! There is an offshoot coming from one of the roots and it is putting out leaves! I think the Old Elm will survive after all!" The blue-gray eyes were shining as I slipped my arm through his and we turned our steps toward home.

# Epilogue

The Old Elm indeed survived, as shown in this 1872 wood engraving, but it was finally destroyed in a violent storm in 1876. A number of other elm trees in Boston Common today are believed to have descended from this great tree.

# Historical Sources

**New York**
*American Leonardo: the Life of Samuel F. B. Morse*, Carleton Mabee (1943)
*The Columbia Historical Portrait of New York*, John Kouwenhoven (1953)
*Dewitt Clinton*, Dorothie Bobbe (1933)
*The Diary of Philip Hone, 1828-1851*, ed. Allan Nevins (1927)
*The Epic of New York City,* Edward Robb Ellis (1966)
*The Essential New Yorker: Gulian Verplanck*, Robert July (1951)
*Gotham Yankee: William Cullen Bryant*, Harry Peckham (1958)
*In Old New York*, Thomas A Janvier (1968)
*James Fenimore Cooper,* Henry Walcott Boynton (1931)
*Literary New York*, Susan Edmiston & Linda Cirino (1976)
*Mirror for Gotham*, Bayrd Still (1956)
*Reminiscences of an Octogenarian*, Charles Haswell (1896)
*The Story of New York*, Susan Lyman (1964)
*Story of Old New York*, Henry Collins Brown (1934)
*This Was New York*, Frank Monaghan & Marvin Lowenthal (1943)
*Washington Irving: an American Study*, William L. Hedges (1965)
*William Cullen Bryant*, Charles H. Brown (1971)

**Leipzig**
*Clara Schumann: a Dedicated Spirit,* Jean Chissell (1983)
*Clara Schumann: a Romantic Biography,* John Burk (1940)
*Concerto: the story of Clara Schumann,* Bertita Harding (1961)
*The Girlhood of Clara Schumann,* Florence May (1912)
*Mendelssohn and his Times,* Heinrich Jacob (1963)
*On Wings of Song: a Biography of Felix Mendelssohn,* Wilfrid Blunt (1974)
*Robert Schumann: His Life and Work,* Herbert Bedford (1925)
*The Romance of the Mendelssohns,* Jacques Petitpierre (1947)
*Schumann: His Life and Times,* Tim Dowley (1982)

**Boston**
*American Literary Masters,* Vol. I, ed. Charles R. Anderson (1965)
*Charles Eliot Norton,* Kermit Vanderbilt (1959)
*The Culture Factory: Boston Public Schools 1789-1860,* Stanley K. Schultz (1973)
*Edward Everett Hale: a Biography,* Jean Holloway (1956)
*Fifty Years of Music in Boston,* Honor McCusker (1938)
*The Flowering of New England 1815-1865,* Van Wyck Brooks (1936)
*Handel and Haydn Society,* ed. Fred P. Bacon and Edward O. Skelton (1903)
*Hawthorne,* Henry James (1879)
*History of the Handel and Haydn Society,* (Charles C. Perkins 1883)
*Horace Mann: A Biography,* Jonathan Messerli (1972)
*Horace Mann Educational Statesman,* E. I. F. Williams (1937)
*James Russell Lowell and His Friends,* Edward Everett Hale (1899)
*The Life of Margaret Fuller,* Madeline Stern (1942)
*Longfellow: A Full-Length Portrait,* Edward Wagenknecht (1955)
*Longfellow: His Life and Work,* Newton Arvin (1963)

*Margaret Fuller*, Katherine Anthony (1920)
*Margaret Fuller: From Transcendentalism to Revolution*, Paula Blanchard (1978)
*Nathaniel Hawthorne in His Times*, James R. Mellow (1980)
*Notes on Music in Old Boston*, William A. Fisher (1918)
*Old Cambridge*, Thomas Wentworth Higginson (1900)
*Parnassus Corner: a Life of James T. Fields, Publisher to the Victorians*, W. S. Tryon (1963)
*The Peabody Sisters of Salem*, Louise Hall Tharp (1950)
*The Rebellious Puritan: Portrait of Mr. Hawthorne*, Lloyd Morris (1955)
*Then and Now in Education*, Otis W. Caldwell & Stuart A. Courtis (1925)
*Three Wise Virgins*, Gladys Brooks (1957)
*Until Victory: Horace Mann and Mary Peabody*, Louise Hall Tharp (1953)
*Young Longfellow*, Lawrance Thompson (1938)

**General Art and Music**
*The Art-Makers of Nineteenth Century America*, Russell Lynes (1970)
*The Great Pianists*, Harold C. Schonberg (1963)
*The History of American Music*, Louis C. Elson (1915)
*The Lives of the Piano*, ed. James R. Gaines (1981)
*Men, Women and Pianos*, Arthur Loesser (1954)
*Music in America*, Frederic Ritter (1970)
*Music in the United Sates: a Historical Introduction*, H. Wiley Hitchcock (1974)
*Patrons and Patriotism*, Lillian B. Miller (1966)
*Pianos and Their Makers*, Alfred Dolge (1972)
*Steinway*, Ronald V. Ratcliffe (1989)

# About the Author

Jerry Priest is a native Texan, Houstonian since childhood and a graduate of Rice University with a BA in History. Her interest in music dates back to her study of piano both as a child and as an adult. A long-time supporter of the Houston Symphony, she served on the Symphony Board and founded and chaired for the first eleven years the Ima Hogg National Young Artist Competition, now in its 35th year.

**A Barren Landscape** was written in the early 1990s, thereafter to languish on a closet shelf until her son-in-law rescued it and guided it to publication. Jerry also authored several editorial pieces for the *Houston Chronicle* during the 90s.